William Oldys, James Yeowell

A Literary Antiquary - Memoir of William Oldys

Together with his diary, choice notes from his Adversaria, and an account of the

London libraries

William Oldys, James Yeowell

A Literary Antiquary - Memoir of William Oldys
Together with his diary, choice notes from his Adversaria, and an account of the London libraries

ISBN/EAN: 9783337123499

Printed in Europe, USA, Canada, Australia, Japan

Cover: Foto ©Raphael Reischuk / pixelio.de

More available books at **www.hansebooks.com**

A LITERARY ANTIQUARY.

MEMOIR

OF

WILLIAM OLDYS, ESQ.

NORROY KING-AT-ARMS.

Together with

HIS DIARY,

CHOICE NOTES FROM HIS ADVERSARIA,

AND AN

ACCOUNT OF THE LONDON LIBRARIES.

[REPRINTED FROM NOTES AND QUERIES.]

LONDON:

Printed by

SPOTTISWOODE & CO., NEW-STREET SQUARE.

1862.

CONTENTS.

MEMOIR OF WILLIAM OLDYS, ESQ.

Norroy King-at-Arms.

———◆———

THE life of a literary antiquary is seldom sufficiently diversified to afford to a biographer many
materials for his pen, so as to give interest and
vivacity to the historic page. From the noiseless
tenor of his daily pursuits, and the habit he has acquired of holding communion with the past rather
than with the present, his existence is, generally
speaking, subject to fewer vicissitudes than those
which mark the mortal progress of persons belonging to the more active professions : —

> " Allow him but his plaything of a pen,
> He ne'er cabals or plots like other men."

Respecting the parentage of William Oldys there
is some obscurity. Mr. John Taylor, the son of
Oldys's intimate friend, informs us that " Mr.
Oldys was, I understood, the natural son of a
gentleman named Harris, who lived in a respectable style in Kensington Square. How he came
to adopt the name of Oldys, or where he received
his education, I never heard." * All his biographers, however, speak of him as the natural
son of Dr. William Oldys, Chancellor of Lincoln
(from 1683 till his death in 1708), Commissary of
St. Catharine's, Official of St. Alban's, and Advo-

---

* *Records of my Life*, i. 25, ed. 1832.

a

cate of the Admiralty. That even grave civilians
will sometimes deviate from moral purity, is de-
plored by Dr. Coote, who had been informed that
Dr. Oldys "maintained a mistress in a very penurious and private manner." *

The civilian died early in the year 1708, and
in his will he "devises to his loving cozen Mrs.
Ann Oldys his two houses at Kensington, with
the residue of his property," and "appoints the
said Ann Oldys whole and sole executrix of his
Will." It has been conjectured, with some degree of probability, that under the cognomen of
cozen is meant the mother of our literary antiquary; more especially as we find from the will
of the said Ann Oldys, that after two or three
trifling bequests, she "gives all her estate, real
and personal, to her loving friend, Benjamin
Jackman of the said Kensington, upon trust, for
the benefit of her son William Oldys, and she
leaves the tuition and guardianship of her son
William Oldys, during his minority, to the said
Benjamin Jackman." The Will is dated March
21, 1710; and proved by Benjamin Jackman on
April 10, 1711, when our antiquary was in the
fifteenth year of his age.

At the end of a pedigree of the Oldys family
in the handwriting of William Oldys, now in the
British Museum (Addit. MS. 4240 †, p. 14), is
the following entry: "Dr. William Oldys, Ad-
vocate General, born at Addesbury 1636; died at
Kensington, 1708; Duxit Theodosia Lovet, Fil.
Dom. Jo: Halsey: [Issue] William, nat. July
14, 1696." That the Doctor married Theodosia
Lovett there can be no doubt; for not only is
it stated by Burke, that "Robert Lovett, of Lis-

---

* *Lives and Characters of eminent English Civilians*,
p. 95, ed. 1804.
† The same volume contains a long account of Dr.
William Oldys, and other biographical notices of the
family.

combe in Bucks, married Theodosia, daughter of Sir John Halsey, Knt., of Great Gaddesden, Herts; he died *s. p.* in 1683, æt. 26," (*Extinct Baronetage*, ed. 1844, p. 325), but in a pedigree in the College of Arms, dated 1700, and subscribed by Dr. Oldys, his marriage with Theodosia Lovett is duly recorded. While as the Doctor there describes himself as "sine prole," and omits all mention of William Oldys in his will, but leaves to Oldys's mother the property which he eventually inherited, there can be little doubt that the baston ought properly to have figured in the arms of the future Norroy. That Oldys always claimed the civilian for his father, appears from the following note in his annotated Langbaine, p. 131: "To search the old papers in one of my large deal boxes for Mr. Dryden's letter of thanks to my father for some communications relating to Plutarch, when they and others were publishing a translation of all Plutarch's *Lives* in 5 vols. 8vo, 1683. It is copied in the yellow book for Dryden's Life, in which there are about 150 transcriptions, in prose and verse, relating to the life, character, and writings of Mr. Dryden." Pompey the Great was the Life translated by Dr. William Oldys.

William Oldys, the son, was born July 14, 1696, and by the death of his parents was left to make his way in life by his own natural abilities. From his *Autobiography* we learn that he was one of the sufferers in the South Sea Bubble, which exploded in 1720, and involved him in a long and expensive lawsuit. From the year 1724 to 1730 he resided in Yorkshire, and spent most of his time at the seat of the first Earl of Malton, with whom he had been intimate in his youth. In 1725, Oldys, being at Leeds soon after the death of Ralph Thoresby, the antiquary, paid a visit to his celebrated Museum.* As he remained in

---

* *Life of Sir Walter Ralegh*, p. xxxi. ed. 1736.

Yorkshire for about six years, it is not improbable
that he assisted Dr. Knowler in the editorship of
the *Earl of Strafforde's Letters*, &c. 2 vols. fol.
published in 1739. In 1729, he wrote an "Essay
on Epistolary Writings, with respect to the Grand
Collection of Thomas Earl of Strafford. Inscribed
to the Lord Malton." The MS. was probably of
some utility to his Lordship, and his Chaplain,
Dr. Knowler.*

It was during Oldys's visit to Wentworth House
that he became an eye-witness to the destruction
of the collections of the antiquary Richard Gascoyne, consisting of seven great chests of manuscripts. Of this remorseless act of vandalism our
worthy antiquary has left on record some severe
strictures. Here is his account of this literary
holocaust : —

" Richard Gascoyne, Esq., was of kin to the Wentworth
family, which he highly honoured by the elaborate genealogies he drew thereof, and improved abundance of
other pedigrees in most of our ancient historians, and
particularly our topographical writers and antiquaries in
personal history, as Brooke, Vincent, Dugdale, and many
others, out of his vast and most valuable collection of
deeds, evidences, and ancient records, &c., which after
his death, about the time of the Restoration, when he was
about eighty years of age, fell with great part of his
library to the possession of William, the son of Thomas
the first Earl of Strafford, who preserved the books in
his library at Wentworth Woodhouse in Yorkshire, and
the said MSS. in the stone tower there among the family
writings, where they continued safe and untouched till
1728, when Sir Tho. Watson Wentworth †, newly made or

---

* This MS. is also noticed in Oldys's *Dissertation upon
Pamphlets*, p. 561.

† Thomas Wentworth of Wentworth Woodhouse, created Baron Malton 28 May, 1728; Baron of Wath and
Harrowden, Viscount Higham, and Earl of Malton 19
Nov. 1734; became Baron of Rockingham in Feb. 1746,
and was created Marquis of Rockingham 19 April, 1746;
died at Wentworth House 14 Dec. 1750, and was buried
in the Minster at York. *Vide* the pedigree of the family
in Hunter's *Doncaster*, ii. 91.

about to be made Earl of Malton, and to whose father
the said William Earl of Strafford left his estate, burnt
them all wilfully in one morning. I saw the lamentable
fire feed upon six or seven great chests full of the said
deeds, &c., some of them as old as the Conquest, and
even the ignorant servants repining at the mischievous
and destructive obedience they were compelled to. There
was nobody present who could venture to speak but myself, but the infatuation was insuperable. I urged that
Mr. Dodsworth had also spent his life in making such
collections, and they are preserved to this day with re-
verence to their collector, and that it was out of such
that Sir Wm. Dugdale collected the work which had
done so much honour to the Peerage. I did prevail to
the preservation of some few old rolls and publick grants
and charters, a few extracts of escheats, and a few original letters of some eminent persons and pedigrees of
others, but not the hundredth part of much better things
that were destroyed. The external motive for this destruction seemed to be some fear infused by his attorney,
Sam. Buck of Rotheram (since a justice of peace) a man
who could not read one of those records any more than
his lordship, that something or other might be found out
one time or other by somebody or other—the descendants
perhaps of the late Earl of Strafford, who had been at
war with him for the said estate—which might shake his
title and change its owner. Though it was thought he
had no stronger motive for it than his impatience to pull
down the old tower in which they were reposited, to
make way for his undertaker Ralph Tunnicliffe to pile up
that monstrous and ostentatious heap of a house which
is so unproportionable to the body and soul of the possessor, so these antiquities, as useless lumber, were destroyed too. Of that Richard Gascoyne see more in
Thoresby's *Topography of Leeds,* fol. 1715; in Sir Wm.
Dugdale's *Antiquities of Warwickshire,* where he is ap-
plauded for his revival of the Wentworth family, as he
ought to have been respected by it for the honour which
he, and the profit his kindred, brought to it (p. 554),
how gratefully repaid appears above. Also in Dugdale's
Memoirs of his own Life, in the note I have made upon
Burton's *Leicestershire* (throughout enriched with his
notes), in the *Harleian Catalogue,* vol. iii. p. 23, 8°, 1744.*

---

* Oldys's note is worth quoting, He says, " Throughout this much-esteemed work [Burton's *Leicestershire,*
1622] there have been numberless notes transcribed in
the margins, and almost all the pedigrees enlarged and

Some men have no better way to make themselves the
most conspicuous persons in their family than by de-
stroying the monuments of their ancestors, and raising
themselves trophies out of their ruins."

We get a glimpse of Oldys's literary habits at
this time from the following note : —

"When I left London in 1724 to reside in Yorkshire,
I left in the care of Mr. Burridge's family, with whom I
had several years lodged, among many other books, goods,
&c. a copy of this Langbaine, in which I had written
several notes and references to further knowledge of these
poets. When I returned to London in 1730, I understood my books had been dispersed ; and afterwards be-

corrected, from a copy of this book in the library of Jesus
College, Cambridge. It has been new bound, and interleaved also throughout, to make room for any further
additions. The notes aforesaid were written by one of
the most skilful antiquaries in Record-heraldry of his
times (as T. Fuller has justly distinguished him), Richard
Gascoyne, Esq., of Bramham Biggen in Yorkshire. He
was a descendant from Judge Gascoyne (who committed
the Prince of Wales, afterwards King Henry V., to prison
for obstructing him in the course of justice on the King's
Bench), and was also related to the first Earl of Strafford, whose grandfather married one of his family. Part
of his pedigree may be seen in Mr. Thoresby's *Antiquities
of Leeds.* He did singular honours to that Earl's name,
in the most elaborate Tables of Genealogy which he drew
out of a vast treasure of original charters, patents, evidences, wills, and other records, which he had amassed
together ; for which, and other such performances, he is
highly praised by Sir Wm. Dugdale in his *Antiquities of
Warwickshire,* and in his *Account of his own Life.* But
how that treasure of Records was wilfully burnt, about the
year 1728 need not to be remembered here. That he was
the author of the notes in this book (as he was of the
like in many other books of our genealogical and topographical antiquities) appears on page 35, and in other
parts of the book, that he wrote them in the year 1656,
at which time he was seventy-seven years of age. He
was born at Sherfield, near Burntwood, in Essex, and
died, it is probable, at Bramham Biggen aforesaid, before
the Restoration." Oldys has also given a digest of Burton's *Leicestershire* in the *British Librarian,* pp 287—
299.

coming acquainted with Mr. Thomas Coxeter, I found that he had bought my Langbaine of a bookseller, who was a great collector of plays and poetical books: this must have been of service to him, and he has kept it so carefully from my sight, that I never could have the opportunity of transcribing into this I am now writing in, the notes I had collected in that." *

In October, 1728, Mr. Henry Baker, the naturalist, under the assumed name of Henry Stonecastle, projected *The Universal Spectator*, to which periodical Oldys, in 1731, had contributed about twenty papers.† On his return to London, in 1730, he found Samuel Burroughs, Esq. and others engaged in a project for printing *The Negotiations of Sir Thomas Roe*. To assist in so desirable an undertaking, Oldys drew up " Some Considerations upon the Publication of Sir Thomas Roe's Epistolary Collections." ‡

It was about the year 1731 that Oldys became acquainted with that noble patron of literature and learned men, Edward Harley, the second Earl of Oxford. It has been wisely and beautifully said, that " those who befriend genius when it is struggling for distinction, befriend the world, and their names should be held in remembrance." We learn from his *Autobiography*, that Oldys must already have become, to some extent, a collector of literary curiosities. He says,

---

* Langbaine in British Museum with Oldys's MS. notes, p. 353.

† *The Universal Spectator* continued to appear weekly until the latter end of the year 1742. In 1736 a selection from these papers was first printed in 2 vols. 12mo; a second edition appeared in 1747, in 4 vols. 12mo; and a third in 1756, in 4 vols. 12mo. John Kelly, the dramatic poet, and Sir John Hawkins, were occasional contributors.

‡ Only one volume of the *Negotiations* was published in 1740. Oldys's " Considerations " for their publication is in the British Museum, Addit. MS. 4168. Vide *postea*, p. 3, and Bolton Corney's *Curiosities of Literature Illustrated*, second edition, 1838, p. 165.

" The Earl invited me to show him my collections of manuscripts, historical and political, which had been the Earl of Clarendon's; my collections of Royal Letters, and other papers of State; together with a very large collection of English heads in sculpture, which alone had taken me some years to collect, at the expense of at least threescore pounds. All these, with the catalogues I drew up of them, at his Lordship's request, I parted with to him for 40*l.*; and the frequent intimations he gave me of a more substantial recompense hereafter, which intimations induced me to continue my historical researches, as what would render me most acceptable to him." — *Autobiography.*

Oldys likewise informs us, in a note on Langbaine, that he had bought two hundred volumes at the auction of the Earl of Stamford's library in St. Paul's Coffee-house, where formerly most of the celebrated libraries were sold.

That Oldys has already become a diligent student at the Harleian Library is evident from the publication at this time of his very curious work on Pamphlets. It first appeared with the following title : *A Dissertation upon Pamphlets. In a Letter to a Nobleman* [probably the Earl of Oxford]. London : Printed in the year 1731, 4to. In the following year it re-appeared in Morgan's *Phœnix Britannicus*, Lond. 1732, 4to ; and has since been reprinted in Nichols's *Literary Anecdotes*, iv. 98—111. Oldys also contributed to the *Phœnix Britannicus*, p. 65, a bibliographical history of " A Short View of the long Life and Raigne of Henry the Third, King of England : presented to King James by Sir Robert Cotton, but not printed till 1627."

It is stated by Dr. Ducarel that Oldys was one of the writers in *The Scarborough Miscellany*, 1732-34. This appears probable, as John Taylor, the author of *Monsieur Tonson,* informed Mr. Isaac D'Israeli that " Oldys always asserted that he was the author of the well-known song —

' Busy, curious, thirsty fly ! '

And as he was a rigid lover of truth, I doubt
not that he wrote it." The earliest version of it
discovered by Mr. D'Israeli was in a collection
printed in 1740 ; but it had appeared in *The
Scarborough Miscellany* for 1732, eight years
earlier. As it slightly varies from the version
quoted by D'Israeli, we give it as originally
printed : —

" THE FLY.

"*An Anacreontick.*

" Busy, curious, thirsty Fly,
Gently drink, and drink as I ;
Freely welcome to my Cup,
Could'st thou sip, and sip it up ;
Make the most of Life you may,
Life is short and wears away.

" Just alike, both mine and thine,
Hasten quick to their Decline ;
Thine's a Summer, mine's no more,
Though repeated to threescore ;
Threescore Summers when they're gone,
Will appear as short as one." *

The London booksellers, having decided on
publishing a new edition of Sir Walter Ralegh's
History of the World, enlisted the services of
Oldys to see it through the press. To this edition is prefixed " The Life of the Author, newly
compil'd, from Materials more ample and authen-
tick than have yet been publish'd, by Mr. Oldys."
The Life makes 282 pages, and from the authorities quoted in the numerous notes must have
been a task of considerable labour and research.

_____

* Ritson has printed " The Fly " in his *English Songs*,
and added the following note : " Made extempore by a
gentleman, occasioned by a fly drinking out of his cup of
ale." In Park's edition of Ritson's *Songs*, ii. 19, edit.
1813, a third verse is added from the Rev. Mr. Plumptre's
Collection of Songs, i. 257 ; and in Hone's *Table Book*, ii. 592,
it appears with five additional verses. Vincent Bourne's
translation was first printed in the Appendix to the third
edition to his *Poems*, 1743. After all, there is an uncer-
tainty respecting its authorship.

The complete work is in two volumes, fol. 1736, and contains a very copious Index. Gibbon meditated a Life of Ralegh; but after reading Oldys's, he relinquished his design, from a conviction that "he could add nothing new to the subject, except the uncertain merit of style and sentiment."
While engaged on this great work, Oldys was permitted to consult the valuable library of Sir Hans Sloane, as we learn from the following letter to the worthy baronet, dated Sept. 29, 1735:—

"MOST HONOURED SIR,

"When I was last favoured, through your noble courtesy, with a sight of some curious Memorials relating to Sir Walter Ralegh, I said there would be one or two little printed pieces which I should have occasion to make more use of than I could take the liberty of doing in your house. One of them, however, which is the *Life of Mahomet*, I have been since provided with; but the other, called *News of Sir Walter Ralegh*, &c., printed 4º, 1618, and marked among the MSS. B. 1288, is now, that I am arrived (through above forty sheets) at the last two years of his Life, immediately wanting.

"As a troublesome cold confines me a little at present, I shall take it as the greater favour if you will let me have it, when it may be most convenient, by the bearer; and I shall, in two or three weeks, wait on you with it again; as also, with an entire copy from the press, of that Narrative which it will help to illustrate. If it may not be too ambitious in me to make so much addition to your library, it may exalt the fame of my Worthy, or extend the date of it, to have his Life preserved in such a magnificent repository, notwithstanding the defects of
             "Honoured Sir,
             "Your most obliged and obedient Servant,
                         "WILLIAM OLDYS."*

Soon after the publication of the *Life of Sir Walter Ralegh*, some booksellers thinking Oldys's name would tend to sell a work then in the course of publication, offered him a considerable sum of money, if they would allow him to affix it; but he rejected the proposal with the greatest indigna-

---

* Addit. MS. 4054, p. 250, Brit. Museum.

tion, though at the time he was in the greatest
pecuniary distress.

At the commencement of the last century Bibliography as a science had not been cultivated in
England. Sale-catalogues and lists of books, especially when interspersed with remarks of their
rarity and value, were collected and prized by
bibliographers ; but Oldys was among the first in
this country to make an attempt to divert the
public taste from an exclusive attention to new
books, by making the merit of old ones the subject of critical discussion.* His *Life of Ralegh*
had not only brought him into closer ties of friendship with the Earl of Oxford ; but the knowledge
of our earliest English literature displayed in
that work had so increased his fame, that he was
now frequently consulted at his chambers in
Gray's Inn on obscure and obsolete writers by the
most eminent literary characters of the time. It
redounds to the honour and memory of William
Oldys that he was ever easy of access to all who
sought or desired his assistance, and free, open,
and communicative in answering the inquiries
submitted to him. His friendly aid and counsel
were not only cheerfully rendered to Thomas
Hayward for his *British Muse*, and to Mrs. Cooper
for *The Muses' Library*, but even his jottings for
a Life of Nell Gwyn were freely given to the
notorious Edmund Curll, whose fame will never
die, gibbeted as he has been to immortality in
the full blazon of his literary knavery.

---

* The only treatise on Bibliography which had appeared in this country, was the erudite work of Sir
Thomas Pope Blount, entitled " Censura Celebriornm
Authorum : sive Tractatus, in quo varia Virorum Doc-
torum de clarissimis cujusque Sæculi Scriptoribus judi-
cia traduntur." Lond. 1690, fol. Isaac Reed informs us,
that Heber's copy of this book came out of the library of
William Oldys, by whom all the manuscript additions
were made. *Vide* Heber's *Catalogue*, part iv. lot 156.

In 1737 Oldys published anonymously his celebrated work, entitled

"The British Librarian: exhibiting a Compendious Review or Abstract of our most scarce, useful, and valuable Books in all Sciences, as well in Manuscript as in Print: with many Characters, Historical and Critical, of the Authors, their Antagonists, &c., in a manner never before attempted, and useful to all readers. With a Complete Index to the volume. London: Printed for T. Osborne, in Gray's-Inn, 1738, 8vo."

It was published as a serial in six numbers; No. I. is dated for January, 1737; and the last, No. VI. for June, 1737; but yet the Postscript at the end of it is signed "Gray's Inn, Feb. 18, 1737 [1737-8]. Some copies have separate titles to the six numbers. The work is highly valuable as containing many curious details of works now excessively rare. Had it been continued, it would, in all probability, have contained an accurate account of a very curious and valuable collection of English books: it ceased, however, at the end of the sixth monthly number, when Mr. Oldys could neither be persuaded by the entreaty of his friends, nor the demands of the public, to continue the labour. Dr. John Campbell, in his *Rational Amusement*, 8vo, 1754, says, that no work of the kind was so well received; and adds, "If its author, who is of all men living the most capable, would pursue and perfect this plan, he would do equal justice to the living and to the dead." "The *British Librarian*," remarks Dr. Dibdin, "is a work of no common occurrence, or mean value. It is rigidly correct, if not very learned, in bibliographical information. I once sent three guineas to procure a copy of it, according to its description, upon *large paper*; but on its arrival I found it to be not quite so large as my own tolerably amply-margined copy."—(*Bibliomania*, p. 52, edit. 1842.)

It may seem to many a very meagre and unsatisfactory labour to compile a chronological

Catalogue of standard works, intermixed with remarks and characters. But (as Oldys cites from Lord Bacon) "learned men want such inventories of every thing in art and nature, as rich men have of their estates." When we first enter on any branch of study, it is palpably useful to have the authors to whom we should resort pointed out to us. "Through the defect of such intelligence, in its proper extent," says Oldys, "how many authors have we, who are consuming their time, their quiet, and their wits, in searching after either what is past finding, or already found? In admiring at the penetrations themselves have made, though to the rind only, in those very branches of science which their forefathers have pierced to the pith? And how many who would be authors as excellent as ever appeared, had they but such plans or models laid before them as might induce them to marshal their thoughts into a regular order; or did they but know where to meet with concurrence of opinion, with arguments, authorities, or examples, to corroborate and ripen their teeming conceptions?"

In the Postscript to this valuable work Oldys thus acknowledges his obligations to his literary friends for the loan of manuscripts and other rare books : —

"Among the books conducive to this purpose, those for which gratitude here demands chiefly the publication of our thanks, are the manuscripts. Such, in the first place, is that here called Sir Thomas Wriothesly's Collections; containing the arms and characters of the Knights of the Garter, and views of the ancient ceremonies used in creating the Knights of the Bath, &c. For that sketch which the Librarian has here given the publick of it, they are both beholden to the permission of his Grace the Duke of Montagu, the noble owner of that valuable volume; and to some explanations thereof, which were also courteously imparted by John Anstis, Esq., Garter, principal King of Arms, whose extensive knowledge in these subjects, his own elaborate publications, in honour

b

of both those Orders, have sufficiently confirm'd.   Nor
will it be thought a repetition unnecessary, by grateful
minds, that the Librarian here renews his acknowledgments to Nathaniel Booth, Esq. of Gray's Inn, for his
repeated communications; having been favour'd not only
with that curious miscellany, containing many of the
old Earl of Derby's papers, which, in one of the foregoing
numbers is abridg'd; but others out of his choice collections, which may enrich some future numbers, when opportunity shall permit the contents thereof to appear,
Other manuscripts herein described, were partly the collection of Mr. Charles Grimes, late also of Gray's Inn,
and in the bookseller's possession for whom this work is
printed; except one ancient relique of the famous Wick-
life, for the use of which, many thanks are here return'd
to Mr. Joseph Ames, Member of the Society of Antiquaries.   The author of this work is moreover obliged to the
library of this last worthy preserver of antiquities, as
also to that of his ingenious friend Mr. Peter Thompson,
for the use of several printed books which are more scarce
than many manuscripts; particularly some, set forth by
our first printer in England; and others, which will rise,
among the curious, in value, as, by the depredations of
accident or ignorance, they decrease in number.   We
must take some further opportunity to express our obligations to other gentlemen who have favour'd us with
such like literary curiosities; and to some hundreds unknown, who have shewn a relish for the usefulness of this
performance, by encouraging the sale of it."

Humphry Wanley, the learned librarian of the
first two Earls of Oxford, had now been dead
more than ten years, and Oldys was probably
expecting to be nominated his successor. Such an
appointment, with a fixed salary, would relieve him
from all perplexity in domestic matters, and would
be therefore infinitely more congenial to his retired habits of life, than the precarious, and in
some cases, paltry remuneration received from the
booksellers. He thus expresses his own feelings
at this time : —

"In the latter end of the year 1737 I published my
British Librarian; and when his Lordship understood
how unproportionate the advantages it produced were to
the time and labour bestowed upon it, he said he would
find me employment better worth my while. Also, when

he heard that I was making interest with Sir Robert Walpole, through the means of Commissioner Hill, to present him with an abstract of some ancient deeds I had relating to his ancestors, and which I have still, his Lordship induced me to decliue that application, saying, though he could not do as grand things as Sir Robert, he would do that which might be as agreeable to me, if I would disengage myself from all other persons and pursuits." — *Autobiography.*

In the following year the Earl of Oxford appointed him his literary secretary, which afforded him an opportunity of consulting his extensive collections, and thus gratifying his predilection for bibliographical researches. During his brief connection with this " Ark of Literature," he frequently met at the Earl's table George Vertue, Alexander Pope, and other eminent literary characters. These three short years may be regarded as among the most happy of his chequered existence. We have from his own pen the following plaintive record of his daily pursuits at this time :

"I had then also had, for several years, some dependence upon a nobleman, who might have served me in the government, and had, upon certain motives, settled an annuity upon me of twenty pounds a year. This I resigned to the said nobleman for an incompetent considaration, and signed a general release to him, in May, 1738, that I might be wholly independent, and absolutely at my Lord Oxford's command. I was likewise then under an engagement with the undertakers of the *Supplement to Bayle's Dictionary.** I refused to digest the materials I then had for this work under an hundred pounds a year, till it was finished; but complied to take forty shillings a sheet for what I should write, at such intervals as my business would permit: for this clause I was obliged to insert in the articles then executed between them and myself, in March the year aforesaid ; whereby I reserved myself free for his lordship's service. And though I pro-

---

* By the Supplement to Bayle's *Dictionary* is meant *A General Dictionary, Historical and Critical,* Lond. 1734-41, fol., 10 vols., and which included that of Bayle. Dr. Birch was the principal editor, assisted by the Rev. John Peter Bernard, John Lockman, and George Sale.

posed, their said offer would be more profitable to me
than my own, yet my lord's employment of me, from that
time, grew so constant, that I never finished above three
or four lives for that work, to the time of his death. All
these advantages did I thus relinquish, and all other dependence, to serve his lordship. And now was I employed at auctions, sales, and in writing at home, in
transcribing my own collections or others for his lordship, till the latter part of the year 1739; for which
services I received of him about 150 pounds. In November the same year I first entered his library of manuscripts,
whereunto I came daily, sorted and methodised his vast
collection of letters, to be bound in many volumes; made
abstracts of them, and tables to each volume; besides
working at home, mornings and evenings, for the said
library. Then, indeed, his lordship, considering what
beneficial prospects and possessions I had given up, to
serve him, and what communications I voluntarily made
to his library almost every day, by purchases which I
never charged, and presents out of whatever was most
worthy of publication among my own collections, of
which he also chose what he pleased, whenever he came
to my chambers, which I have since greatly wanted, I
did thenceforward receive of him two hundred pounds
a-year, for the short remainder of his life. Notwithstanding this allowance, he would often declare in company before me, and in the hearing of those now alive,
that he wished I had been some years sooner known to
him than I was; because I should have saved him many
hundred pounds.

"The sum of this case is, that for the profit of about
500*l.* I devoted the best part of ten years' service to, and
in his lordship's library; impoverished my own stores to
enrich the same; disabled myself in my studies, and the
advantages they might have produced from the publick;
deserted the pursuits which might have obtained me a
permanent accommodation; and procured the prejudice
and misconceit of his lordship's surviving relations. But
the profits I received were certainly too inconsiderable to
raise any envy or ill will; tho' they might probably be
conceived much greater then they were. No, it was what
his lordship made me more happy in, than his money,
which has been the cause of my greatest unhappiness
with them; his favour, his friendly reception and treat-
ment of me; his many visits at my chambers; his many
invitations by letters, and otherwise, to dine with him
and pass whole evenings with him; for no other end, but
such intelligence and communications, as might answer

the inquiries wherein he wanted to be satisfied, in relation
to matters of literature, all for the benefit of his library.
Had I declined those invitations. I must, with great ingratitude, have created his displeasure; and my accept-
ance of them has displeased others."

It is painful to record, that the Earl of Oxford,
when Oldys entered his service, had involved
himself in pecuniary difficulties whilst collecting
one of the choicest and most magnificent private
libraries in this kingdom. Vertue, in one of his
Commonplace-books, under the date of June 2,
1741, thus feelingly laments the embarrassed circumstances of the Earl : —

" My good Lord, lately growing heavy and pensive on
his affairs, which for some years has mortified his mind.
It lately manifestly appeared in his change of complexion,
his face fallen; his colour and eyes turned yellow to a
great degree; his stomach wasted and gone; and a dead
weight presses continually, without sign of relief, on his
mind. Yet through all his affliction I am, from many
reasons and circumstances, sensible of his goodness and
generosity to those about him that deserved his favour.
I pray God restore his health and preserve him: it will
be a great comfort to his good lady, her Grace his daughter, and all his relations and obliged friends."

A fortnight afterwards Vertue thus pathetically
laments his loss : —

"The Creator of all has put an end to his life. The
true, noble, and beneficent Edward Earl of Oxford and
Earl Mortimer, Baron of Wigmore, born 2nd of June,
1688, and died the 16th of June, 1741. A friend noble,
generous, good, and amiable; to me, above all men, a true
friend : the loss not to be expressed." *

We have seen that Oldys's salary as librarian
was 200l. per annum. At the death of the Earl
he received what was due to him, amounting to
about three quarters of a year's exhibition, on
which he lived so long as it lasted. His prospects
at this time must have been gloomy indeed, for he
was again compelled to renew his connection with
the metropolitan publishers. For the next four-

* Addit. MS. 23,093, pp. 22, 23.

b 3

teen years, until he received an appointment in
the Heralds' Office, he continued to earn his
bread by literary drudgery for the booksellers.
His scattered fragments of ancient lore that have
escaped the ravages of time are a proof of his laborious application in literary researches: his pen
was continually at work either in writing pamphlets, prefaces, essays, or in his favourite pursuit,
biographical memoirs. " Some men," says Dean
Swift, " know books as they do lords ; learn their
titles exactly, and then brag of their acquaintance:" Not so William Oldys. His abstracts and
critical notices of works of our early English literature in the *British Librarian*, as well as his
other numerous productions, afford a remarkable
proof of his rare industry, intelligence, and wit.

In 1742, Mr. Thomas Osborne the bookseller
having purchased for the sum of 13,000*l.* the collection of printed books that had belonged to the
late Earl of Oxford, and intending to dispose of
them by sale, projected a Catalogue in which it
was proposed, "that the books shall be distributed
into distinct classes, and every class arranged with
some regard to the age of the writers ; that every
book shall be accurately described ; that the peculiarities of editions shall be remarked, and observations from the authors of Literary History
occasionally interspersed, that, by this Catalogue,
posterity may be informed of the excellence and
value of this great Collection, and thus promote
the knowledge of scarce books and elegant editions." The learned Michael Maittaire was pre-
vailed upon to draw out the scheme of arrange-
ment, and to write a Latin Dedication to Lord
Carteret, then Secretary of State. The editors
selected by Osborne were Dr. Johnson and William Oldys, men eminently qualified to carry out
the undertaking.

In this painful drudgery both editors were day-
labourers for immediate subsistence, not unlike

Gustavus Vasa, working in the mines of Dale-carlia. What Wilcox, a bookseller of eminence in the Strand, said to Johnson, on his first arrival in town, was now almost confirmed. He lent him five guineas, and then asked him, "How do you mean to earn your livelihood in this town?" "By my literary labours," was the answer. Wilcox, staring at him, shook his head: "By your literary labours! You had better buy a porter's knot." In fact, Johnson, while employed by Osborne in Gray's Inn, may be said to have carried a porter's knot. He paused occasionally to peruse the book that came to his hand. Osborne thought that such curiosity tended to nothing but delay, and objected to it with all the pride and insolence of a man who knew that he paid daily wages.* Ralph Bigland, Bluemantle, related to John Charles Brooke, Somerset Herald, that "Osborne had informed him, that he would have given Oldys 10*s.* 6*d.* per diem if he would have written for him; but his *indolence* (!) would not let him accept it." † If this offer was made during the compilation of the catalogue, it is evident that the publisher exacted from his editors more work than could possibly be accomplished in a specified time, for the number of books to be read and digested amounted to no less than 20,748 volumes. Hence the failure of the original scheme as judiciously propounded by Maittaire. Our two unfortunate editors, in their joint and seemingly interminable labour, whilst grappling with this solid battalion of printed books, gained little more

---

* Drake's *Essays on Periodical Papers,* i. 157, ed. 1809; and Hawkins's *Life of Dr. Johnson,* p. 150, ed. 1787.

† Notes by John Charles Brooke in his *De vitis Fecia-lium,* a MS. now in the College of Arms. Brooke was appointed Rouge Croix in 1773; and Somerset in 1778; he was not, therefore, a contemporary officer in the college with Oldys.

for their pains than the dust with which (so
long as their drudgery lasted) they were daily
covered.

As literary curiosities, it is now difficult to
discriminate between the notes of Dr. Johnson
and those of Oldys. The " Proposals " for printing the *Bibliotheca Harleiana* are clearly from the
pen of the Doctor, as we are informed by
Boswell, who adds, that " his account of that
celebrated collection of books, in which he displays the importance to literature of what the
French call a *catalogue raisonné*, when the subjects of it are extensive and various, and it is
executed with ability, cannot fail to impress all
his readers with admiration of his philological at-
tainments. It was afterwards prefixed to the first
volume of the Catalogue, in which the Latin accounts of books were written by him."* We incline
to the conjecture that the bibliographical and biographical remarks in Vols. I. and II. are by Dr.
Johnson: and those in Vols. III. and IV. by Oldys.
The fifth volume, 1745, is nothing more than a
Catalogue of Osborne's unsold stock.

Osborne's original project of an annotated Catalogue, as we have said, proved a failure. In the
Preface to Vol. III. he informs the public of its
cause :—

" My original design was, as I have already explained,
to publish a methodical and exact Catalogue of this
library, upon the plan which has been laid down, as I
am informed, by several men of the first rank among the
learned. It was intended by those who undertook the
work, to make a very exact disposition of all the subjects,
and to give an account of the remarkable differences of
the editions, and other peculiarities, which make any
book eminently valuable; and it was imagined, that
some improvements might, by pursuing this scheme, be
made in Literary History. With this view was the Catalogue begun, when the price [5s. per volume] was fixed

---

* It is also printed in the *Gentleman's Magazine* for
Dec. 1742, vol. xii. p. 636.

upon it in public advertisements; and it cannot be denied, that such a Catalogue would have been willingly purchased by those who understood its use. But, when a few sheets had been printed, it was discovered that the scheme was impracticable without more hands than could be procured, or more time than the necessity of a speedy sale would allow. The Catalogue was therefore continued without Notes, at least in the greatest part; and, though it was still performed better than those which are daily offered to the public, fell much below the original design."*

Whilst the Catalogue was progressing, Osborne issued Proposals for printing by subscription *The Harleian Miscellany :* or, a Collection of scarce, curious, and entertaining Tracts and Pamphlets found in the late Earl of Oxford's library, interspersed with Historical, Political, and Critical Notes. It was proposed to publish six sheets of this work every Saturday morning, at the price of one shilling, to commence on the 24th of March, 1743-4. The "Proposals," or "An Account of this Undertaking," as well as the Preface to this voluminous work, were from the pen of Dr. Johnson : the selection of the Pamphlets and its editorial superintendence devolved upon Oldys. This valuable political, historical, and antiquarian record, and indispensable auxiliary in the illustration of British history, included a catalogue of 539 pamphlets, describing the contents of each, and this alone occupied 164 quarto pages. It was published in eight volumes, 4to, 1744-46, and republished by Thomas Park, with two supplemental volumes, in 1808-13. Park, in a letter to Sir Samuel Egerton Brydges, dated June 15, 1807, bears the following honourable testimony to the labours of his predecessor : — " My additions to the notes of Oldys in the *Harleian Miscellany*

---

* The most copiously annotated Catalogue of modern times is that of M. Guglielmo Libri, whose surprising collection was sold by Messrs. Sotheby and Wilkinson in April, May, and July, 1861.

will not be very numerous; for no editor could
ever have been more competent to the undertaking than he was; but a successive editor must
seem at least to have done something more than
his predecessor." *

It was the original intention of the publishers
to print *three* additional volumes to this edition,
though motives afterwards occurred which induced
them to depart from it.   Park, writing to Sir S. E.
Brydges on Jan. 28, 1813, says, " I presume you
have heard from our friend Haslewood that my
projected course in the *Harleian Supplement* has
been suddenly arrested, and that the work is to
stop with vol. X., half of which will be occupied
with Indices.   This has painfully disconcerted my
views, and rendered a considerable portion of my
preparations useless." †

" Next in point of merit to the contributions
of Oldys to British biography," writes our valued
correspondent, MR. BOLTON CORNEY, " must be
placed his publications in bibliography.   Those
which are best known are much esteemed, but there
is one which has never received its due share of
commendation.   It is entitled *A copious and exact
catalogue of pamphlets in the Harleian Library, etc.*
4°, pp. 168.   This catalogue was issued in fragments with the *Harleian Miscellany*, in order to
gratify the subscribers with an opportunity of
being their own choosers with regard to the contents of that important collection; but as the
signatures and numerals are consecutive, it forms
a separate volume.   The pamphlets described
amount to 548.   The dates extend from 1511
to 1712, but about two-thirds of the number were
printed before 1661.   The titles are given with
unusual fulness, and the imprints with sufficient
minuteness.   The number of sheets or leaves of
each pamphlet is also stated.   The subjects em-

---

* Addit. MS. 18,916, p. 21ᵇ.   † Ibid, p. 84.

braced are divinity, voyages and travels, history, biography, polite literature, etc. etc.—A catalogue of books or pamphlets, if it requires a sharp eye, is mere transcription, but in this instance we have about 440 *notes*, of which many are summaries of the contents of the articles in question, drawn up with remarkable intelligence and clearness, and interspersed with curious anecdotes. It is a choice specimen of *recreative bibliography*. Chalmers has omitted to notice this volume, and so has Lowndes. The copy which I possess was formerly in the library of Mr. Isaac Reed, and at the sale of his books in 1807 it was purchased by Mr. Heber for 2*l*. 3*s*. It cost me no more than 8*s*. 6*d*."

A copy of this valuable Catalogue in the library of the Corporation of London formerly belonged to Dr. Michael Lort, who has written the following note in it : " This account was drawn up by the very intelligent Mr. Oldys. It is very seldom to be found compleat in this manner. Many curious particulars of literary and biographical history are to be found in it. I paid 5*s*. for it. Feb. 18, 1772." This Catalogue has been reprinted by Mr. Park in the last edition of the *Harleian Miscellany*, vol. x. pp. 357-471.

After the completion of *The Harleian Miscellany*, it does not appear that Oldys continued much longer in the employ of Thomas Osborne ; at that time the most celebrated publisher in the metropolis. If we may judge from the series of catalogues issued by this bookseller from the year 1738 to 1766, he must have carried on a successful and lucrative trade. These catalogues may now be reckoned among the curiosities of literature ; for nowhere do we meet with similar information respecting the prices of books at that time, or more amusement than in his quaint notes, and still more quaint prefaces. For how many of these curious bibliographical memoranda

he was indebted to his neighbour, William Oldys,
cannot now be ascertained. Osborne's exploits
are thus celebrated in the *Dunciad:* —
   " Osborne and Curll accept the glorious strife,
   Though this his Son dissuades, and that his Wife."

Again, at the conclusion of the contest : —
   " Osborne, through perfect modesty o'ercome,
   Crown'd with the jordan, walks contented home."

Osborne was so impassively dull and ignorant in
what form or language Milton's *Paradise Lost* was
written, that he employed one of his garreteers to
render it from a French translation into English
prose. He is now best known as the bookseller
whom Johnson knocked down with a folio. " Sir,"
said the Doctor to Boswell, " he was impertinent
to me, and I beat him ; but it was not in his shop,
it was in my own chamber." On August 27, 1767,
this bibliopole was buried in the churchyard of
St. Mary, Islington, leaving behind him the com-
fortable assets of 40,000*l.* So true is it what
Walcot said rather strongly, " That publishers
drink their claret out of authors' skulls." But,
as Thomas Park shrewdly observed, " Some might
say, that authors must have paper skulls to suffer
it."

In 1746 was published a new edition of *Health's
Improvement*, by Dr. Moffet, corrected and en--
larged by Christopher Bennet, M.D. Prefixed is
a view of the author's life and writings from the
pen of William Oldys. No copy of this work is to
be found in our national library, and it is omitted
in both editions of Lowndes. With its publication
terminated Oldys's connexion with Osborne.

The editorship of Michael Drayton's *Works*,
fol. 1748, has been attributed to Oldys by a writer in the *Gentleman's Magazine*, vol. lvii. pt. ii.
p. 1081, as well as by Mr. Octavius Gilchrist in
Aikin's *Athenæum*, ii. 347, who adds, " It is not
generally known that these collections [of Dray-

ton's *Works*] were made by Oldys, with less
than his usual accuracy." But from the article
DRAYTON, in the *Biographia Britannica*, ed. 1750,
written by Oldys himself, it appears that he
only furnished the "Historical Essay" prefixed to the edition of Drayton's *Works*, 1748, as
well as to that of 1753. Speaking of the *Barons'
Wars*, Oldys remarks, "In this edition [1748]
these *Barons' Wars* in the reign of Edward II.
are illustrated with marginal notes by the author,
which have been all since omitted by his late
editor, though *the author of the Preliminary Discourse* was desirous of a more ample commen-
tary." (*Biog. Brit.* iii. 1745, ed. 1750, and Kippis's
edition, v. 360.)

ı Oldys now resolved to devote his exclusive attention to his own peculiar department of literature, that of Biography. Hence we find him, for
the next ten years, employed in the desperate and
weary process of excavation, among the over-
whelming piles of documents preserved in the
public and private libraries of the metropolis.
The facilities afforded to biographers and annalists
of modern times, by the catalogues of the British
Museum and the Calendars of the State Paper
Office, were unknown to the literary adventurer
a century ago. To collect materials for any biographical or historical work required then some
sinew and hardihood to encounter the enormous
and almost unmanageable mass of documents from
which truth was to be dug out. Between the
years 1747 and 1760, it appears that Oldys furnished twenty-two articles to the first edition of
the *Biographia Britannica*, which may rank with
some of the most perfect specimens of biography
in the English language. For the following tabu-
lar view of his labours on this important work,
we are indebted to Bolton Corney's *Curiosities of
Literature Illustrated*, Second Edition, 1838, p.
177 :—

" Contributions of W. Oldys to the Biographia Britannica,
London, 1747–66. *Folio,* 7 *Vols.*

Volume and Date.	Name.	Claim to Admission.	No. of Pages.
i. 1747	George Abbot - -	Archbishop of Canterbury	14½
	Robert Abbot - -	Bishop of Salisbury - -	2½
	Sir Thomas Adams -	Lord Mayor of London -	1½
	W. Alexander Earl of Stirline - -	Statesman and Dramatic Writer - - - -	5
	Charles Aleyn - -	Historical Poet - - -	1½
	Edward Allcyn -	Founder of Dulwich College	7½
	William Ames - -	Divine - - - - -	1½
	John Atherton - -	Bishop of Waterford - -	8
	Peter Bales - -	Writing Master - - -	11
ii. 1748	John Bra'ford - -	Protestant Martyr - -	16½
	William Bulleyn -	Physician and Botanist -	9½
	William Caxton -	Printer - - - - -	26½
iii. 1750	Michael Drayton -	Historical & Pastoral Poet	5
	Sir Geo. Etherege -	Dramatic Writer - -	8
	George Farquhar -	Dramatic Writer - -	11
	Sir John Fastolff -	Statesman and Warrior -	10½
	Thomas Fuller -	Historian, &c. - - -	20
	Sir Will. Gascoigne -	Judge - - - - -	13½
iv. 1757	Fulke Greville, Lord Brook - - -	Biographer and Poet - -	12½
	Rich. Hakluyt - -	Naval Historian - -	14
	Wenceslaus Hollar -	Engraver - - - -	8¾
v. 1760	Thomas May - -	Historian and Poet - -	6

" On the execution of the articles," remarks Mr.
Corney, " I submit some short remarks. The life
of Archbishop Abbot is especially commended by
the author of the preface to the work ; and was
reprinted in 1777, 8vo. The life of Edward
Alleyn is also justly characterised by the same
writer as *very curious.* The article on Peter
Bales, if rather discursive, is rich in information ;
and contains, in the notes, a history of writing-
masters. Bulleyn, whose works were formerly
popular, receives due attention. As Gough remarks, Oldys has " *rescued* him *almost from oblivion.*"* Master William Caxton occupies more
than twenty-six pages. Oldys had carefully ex-
amined the chief portion of his rare volumes ; and
Dr. Dibdin admits that his "*performance is in
every respect superior to that of Lewis.*"† The

* *British Topography,* 1780, 4to, i. 133.
† *Typographical Antiquities,* 1810, 4to, p. lxxiv.

account of Drayton and his works is an interesting specimen. Oldys points out the numerous
deficiencies of the splendid edition of 1748 ; and
his information seems to have led to the completion of it. The life of Sir John Fastolff, of which
the first sketch was contributed to the *General
Dictionary* in 1737, is the result of extraordinary
research. The Fastolff of history and the Falstaff
of fiction are ingeniously contrasted. The account of Fuller is compiled with peculiar care ;
and affords a remarkable proof of the extent to
which the writings of an author may be made
contributive to his biography. The *History of the
Worthies of England*, which Oldys frequently consulted, is characterised with much candour ; and
he has very appropriately introduced the substance of a MS. essay on the *toleration of wit on
grave subjects.* Sir William Gascoigne is copiously
historised. Oldys, with his usual ardour in search
of truth, obtained the use of some *Memoirs of the
Family of Gascoigne* from one of the descendants
of Sir William, and a communication from the
Rev. R. Knight, Vicar of Harwood, where he was
buried. The life of the patriotic Hakluyt claims
especial notice. Oldys had pointed out his merit
more than twenty years before ; * and seems never
to have lost sight of him. He has left an admirable memorial of the "*surpassing knowledge and
learning, diligence and fidelity, of this naval historian*" — and it well deserves to be separately
re-published. The account of Hollar and his works
is written with the animation and tact of a connois-
seur. Oldys justly describes him as *ever making
art a rival to nature,* and as a *prodigy of industry.*
He also reviews the graphic collections of his ad-
mirers, from Evelyn to the Duchess of Portland.
The article on May was his last contribution.
He vindicates the *History of the Parliament* from

---

* *Life of Sir W. R.,* p. cix. + *British Librarian,* p. 137.

the aspersions cast on it — in which he is supported by Bishop Warburton, Lord Chatham, &c.
" It may be safely asserted that no one of the
contributors to the *Biographia Britannica* has
produced a richer proportion of *inedited* facts than
William Oldys ; and he seems to have consulted
every species of the more accessible authorities,
from the *Fœdera* of Rymer to the inscription on
a print. His united articles, set up as the text of
Chalmers, would occupy about a thousand octavo
pages."

Oldys's coadjutors on the *Biographia Britan-
nica* were the Rev. Philip Morant, of Colchester ;
Rev. Thomas Broughton, of the Temple Church ;
Dr. John Campbell, of Exeter Change ; Henry
Brougham, of Took's Court, Cursitor Street, Hol-
born ; Rev. Mr. Hinton, of Red Lion Square ;
Dr. Philip Nicols, Fellow of Trinity Hall, Cam-
bridge ; and Mr. Harris of Dublin.

In 1778, when Dr. Kippis undertook the editorship of the second edition of the *Biographia
Britannica*, he became the fortunate possessor of
a portion of Oldys's manuscript biographical collections, purchased for this work by Mr. Thomas
Cadell, one of the publishers. In his Preface
(vol. i. p. xx.) he states, that " To Dr. Percy,
besides his own valuable assistances, we are indebted for directing us to the purchase of a large
and useful body of biographical materials, left by
Mr. Oldys." These biographical materials were
quoted in the articles Arabella Stuart, John Barclay, Mary Beale, W. Browne, Sam. Butler, &c.
Dr. Kippis found also among Oldys's papers,
some notes principally tending to illustrate several
of Butler's allusions in his *Hudibras* to both ancient and modern authors. (*Vide* vol. iii. p. 91.)

From the years 1751 to 1753, it would seem
that Oldys was involved in pecuniary difficulties ;
and being unable to discharge the rent due for his
chambers in Gray's Inn, was compelled to reside

for a lengthened period in the quiet obscurity of the Fleet prison. It was probably during his confinement that the following letters were written to his friend Dr. Thomas Birch : —

"July 22, 1751.

"SIR,—I received last night two guineas by the hand of my worthy and honourable friend Mr. Southwell; for which favour, and much more for the polite and engaging manner of conferring it, besides this incompetent return of my sincere thanks, I have beg'd him to make my acknowledgments more acceptable than in my present confused and disabled state I am capable myself of doing. I have also desired him to intimate how much more I might be obliged to you, if, at your leisure, and where you shall perceive it convenient, you would so represent me to such Honorable friends among your numerous acquaintance, that they may help me towards a removal into some condition, wherein I may no longer remain altogether unuseful to mankind; which would lay an obligation inexpressible upon, Sir,

"Your most obedient humble servant,
"WILLIAM OLDYS."

"August 23ᵈ, 1751.

"SIR, — That favour I before received of you, was beyond whatever the sense of my own deficiencies could suffer me to expect; but much more this, by which, through your favourable representation of me, or my misfortunes, to the Hon. Mr. Yorke, I received five guineas of him, through the hands of the candid and cordial Mr. Southwell. You may justly believe, that my hearty thanks for this benefit are hereby unfeignedly returned to you, and I have endeavoured to return the like to that noble benefactor. But as I cannot make my gratitude so satisfactory to him, as his goodness has been to me, I still want the assistance of a friend, to convey my acknowledgments, more expressively than I can myself: and I think, by what I have already tasted, I may depend upon that friendship from you.

The happiness I have lately received in perusing your life of Spenser * has greatly restored my desire, in this loitering, lingering, useless condition, to such studies.

---

* Dr. Birch had recently published *The Faerie Queene*, with an exact collation of the two original editions; to which are added a Life of the Author, and a Glossary, with plates, 3 vols. 1751, 4to.

c 3

There are very observable passages in it, both ancient
and modern, which I had not before met with ; for which,
and many other memorable incidents in our most illus-
trious ancestors, recovered and rectified by your reviving
hand, if present readers shall be silent in your praise,
those who are unborn will stigmatise their ingratitude,
in the celebration of your industry.

" I remain, Sir,

" Your most obliged and obedient servant,

" WILLIAM OLDYS." *

In 1753, Oldys in conjunction with Mr. John
Taylor, the oculist in Hatton Garden, published
*Observations on the Cure of William Taylor, the
Blind Boy of Ightham, in Kent*, containing also an
address to the Publick for a foundation of an Hos-
pital for the Blind. Prefixed are two letters from
Oldys to Dr. Monsey of Chelsea Hospital, and one
in reply from the Doctor.

Oldys remained in confinement till Mr. Southwell of Cockermouth (brother of the second Lord
Southwell) and his other friends obtained his liberty.† John Taylor, however, has given the
following account of his release : " Oldys, as my
father informed me, lived many years in quiet obscurity in the Fleet prison, but at last was spirited
up to make his situation known to the Duke of
Norfolk ‡ of that time, who received Oldys's letter
while he was at dinner with some friends. The
Duke immediately communicated the contents to
the company, observing that he had long been
anxious to know what had become of an old,
though an humble friend, and was happy, by that
letter, to find that he was still alive. He then
called for his *gentleman* (a kind of humble friend
whom noblemen used to retain under that name
in former days), and desired him to go immediately to the Fleet prison with money for the im-

---

* Addit. MS. 4316, p. 4.

† *Gent. Mag.* vol. liv. pt. i. p. 260.

‡ Edward Howard: ob. 1777.

mediate need of Oldys, to procure an account of
his debts, and to discharge them."*

Soon after the Duke of Norfolk had released
Oldys from his pecuniary difficulties, he procured
for him the situation of Norroy King-at-Arms —
a post peculiarly suited to his love of genealogy.
He was created Norfolk Herald Extraordinary at
the College of Arms by the Earl of Effingham,
Deputy Earl Marshal, on 15th April, 1755, to
qualify him for the office of Norroy, to which
he was appointed by patent the 5th May following. His noble patron generously defrayed the
fees for passing his patent. The Duke had frequently met Oldys in the library of the late Earl
of Oxford, and had perused with much pleasure
his *Life of Sir Walter Ralegh* and his other
works, and considered him sufficiently qualified,
from his literary acquirements, to restore the
drooping reputation of the office of Norroy. Oldys
appointed as his deputy Edward Orme of Chester, better known as the compiler of pedigrees for
families of that county. "The heralds," says
Noble, "had reason to be displeased with Oldys's
promotion to a provincial kingship. The College,
however, will always be pleased with ranking so
good a writer amongst their body."†

John Taylor, author of *Monsieur Tonson*, relates the following anecdote of our Norroy whilst
performing one of his official duties. "On some
occasion, when the King-at-Arms was obliged to
ride on horseback in a public procession, the predecessor of Mr. Oldys in the cavalcade had a proclamation to read, but, confused by the noise of
the surrounding multitude, he made many mistakes, and, anxious to be accurate, he turned
back to every passage to correct himself, and
therefore appeared to the people to be an ignorant
blunderer. When Mr. Oldys had to recite the

---

* *Records of my Life*, i. 26.　† *College of Arms*, p. 421.

same proclamation, though he made, he said, more
mistakes than his predecessor, he read on through
thick and thin, never stopping a moment to correct his errors, and thereby excited the applause
of the people; though he declared that the other
gentleman had been much better qualified for the
duty than himself." *

We ought to apologise for noticing what Mr.
Bolton Corney justly styles "the most contemptible of books," *The Olio*, published from the
refuse papers of the redoubtable Captain Grose
by his eager executor, who happened to be his
bookseller. Even Mr. Isaac D'Israeli acknowledges, that in it "the delineation of Oldys is
sufficiently overcharged for *the nonce*." Grose, as
every one knows, exceedingly enjoyed a joke; but
probably he never conceived that some officious
hand would gather up and publish the *débris* of
his library for his own mercenary advantage.
This despicable production has been quoted as an
authority by nearly every one who has undertaken to give an account of the life of Oldys.

Grose was appointed Richmond Herald by
patent 12th June, 1755, which he resigned in
1763. He was therefore contemporary with Oldys
during the whole period of his connexion with
the Heralds' College, excepting that Oldys was
appointed Norroy in the May preceding.† Oldys,
however, with all his alleged "deep potations in
ale," was a well-informed literary antiquary — or,
as Grose himself confesses, "in the knowledge
of scarce English books and editions he had
no equal;" but unhappily our facetious Richmond Herald, "who cared more for rusty armour
than for rusty volumes," as D'Israeli remarks,
"would turn over these flams and quips to some
confidential friend, to enjoy together a secret
laugh at their literary intimates." Even the story

---

* *Records of my Life*, i. 26.
† Ex inform. T. W. King, York Herald.

told by Grose of the intoxication of Oldys at the
funeral of the Princess Caroline, and the jeopardy
of the crown, is not accurate; for Mr. Noble
assures us, that the crown, when borne at the
funeral of the king or queen, or the coronet at the
burial of a prince or princess, is always carried by
Clarenceux, not Norroy.*   It is also stated in the
ceremonial of the Princess Caroline's funeral, as
printed in *The London Chronicle* of Jan. 5, 1758,
and *Reed's Weekly Journal* of Jan. 7, 1758, that
"Clarenceux, bearing the coronet upon a black
velvet cushion, preceded the body of the princess." †

Oldys was connected with the College of Arms
for nearly five years.   His library was the large
room up one pair of stairs in Norroy's apartments,
in the west wing of the college, where he chiefly
resided, and which was furnished with little else
than books.   His notes were written on slips of
paper, which he afterwards classified and reposited
in small bags suspended about his room.   It was
in this way that he covered several quires of
paper with laborious collections for a complete
Life of Shakspeare; and from these notes Isaac
Reed made several extracts in the Additional
Anecdotes to Rowe's Life of the Bard.

Oldys at this time frequently passed his evenings at the house of John Taylor, the celebrated oculist of Hatton Garden ‡, where he
always preferred the fireside in the kitchen, that

---

* *College of Arms*, p. 421.

† Mr Thompson Cooper, of Cambridge, in "N. &
Q." 2nd S. iii. 514, has stated, that "on turning to a con-
temporaneous account of the funeral, I find that Norroy
did carry the coronet on that occasion."   We have not
been able to trace the authority for this statement.

‡ John Taylor of Hatton Garden was the son of the
celebrated Chevalier Taylor, and father of John Taylor
the author of *Monsieur Tonson*, and editor of *The Sun*
newspaper.

he might not be obliged to mingle with the other
visitors.   He was so particular in his habits, that
he could not smoke his pipe with ease till his
chair was fixed close to a particular crack in the
floor.   " The shyness of Mr. Oldys's disposition,"
says John Taylor, jun., "and the simplicity of his
manners, had induced him to decline an introduction to my grandfather, the Chevalier Taylor, who
was always splendid in attire, and had been used
to the chief societies in every court of Europe;
but my grandfather had heard so much of Mr.
Oldys, that he resolved to be acquainted with
him, and therefore one evening when Oldys was
enjoying his philosophical pipe by the kitchen
fire, the Chevalier invaded his retreat, and without ceremony addressed him in the Latin language.   Oldys, surprised and gratified to find a
scholar in a fine gentleman, threw off his reserve,
answered him in the same language, and the col-
loquy continued for at least two hours; my father,
not so good a scholar, only occasionally interpos-
ing an illustrative remark." *

Oldys's literary labours were now drawing to a
close, his life having extended to nearly threescore years and ten.   His last production was the
Life of Charles Cotton, piscator and poet, prefixed to Hawkins's edition of Walton's *Compleat
Angler*, edit. 1760, which made forty-eight pages.
It was abridged in the later editions.   As we have
elsewhere noticed (*postea*, page 15).   Dr. Towers,
who compiled the Life of COTTON for Kippis's *Biographia Britannica*, has erroneously attributed
Oldys's Life of this poet to our musical knight.
Grose informs us (*Olio*, p. 139), that " among
Oldys's works is a Preface to Izaak Walton's *Angling*."   This Preface was probably no other than
his "Collections" for a Life of Walton.   In his biographical sketch of Charles Cotton he reminds Sir
John Hawkins, that " as Izaak Walton did oblige

* *Records of my Life,* i. 27.

the public with the lives of several eminent men,
it is much that some little historical monument
has not, in grateful retaliation, been raised and
devoted to his memory. The few materials I,
long since, with much search, gathered up concerning him, you have seen, and extracted I hope,
what you found necessary for the purpose I intended them." (Page iv. See also Hawkins's
Life of Walton in the same volume, p. xlviii.)

William Oldys died at his apartments in the
Heralds' College on April 15, 1761, and was
buried on the 19th of the same month in the
north aisle of St. Benet, Paul's Wharf, towards
the upper end.* His friend, John Taylor of Hatton Garden, on the 20th of June, 1761, adminis-
tered as principal creditor, defrayed the funeral
expenses, and obtained possession of his official
regalia, books, and valuable manuscripts. The
original painting of William Oldys, formerly belonging to Mr. Taylor, is now, we believe, in the
possession of Mr. J. H. Burn of Bow Street; an
engraving from it by Balston will be found in
The European Magazine for November, 1796.
He is drawn in a full-dress suit and bag-wig, and
has the complete air of a venerable patrician.
The following punning anagram on his own name,
and made by himself, occurs in one of his manuscripts in the British Museum : —

" In word and *Will I am* a friend to you,
And one friend *Old is* worth a hundred new."

The printed books found in the library of Oldys,
some of them copiously annotated, together with
a portion of his manuscripts, were sold by Thomas

---

* There is a discrepancy respecting the age of Oldys
at the time of his death. On his coffin, as well as in a
document belonging to the Heralds' College, it is stated
to be seventy-two, and in the newspapers of that time,
seventy-four, which would place his birth in 1687 or 1689;
whereas we have in his own handwriting as the date July
14, 1696. *Vide* Addit. MS. 4240, p. 14.

Davies, the bookseller, on April 12, 1762. Mr.
John Taylor, jun., has given the following account of the dispersion of some of his manuscripts.
He says, " Mr. Oldys had engaged to furnish a
bookseller in the Strand, whose name was Walker,
with ten years of the life of Shakspeare unknown
to the biographers and commentators, but he
died, and 'made no sign' of the projected work.
The bookseller made a demand of twenty guineas
on my father, alleging that he had advanced that
sum to Mr. Oldys, who had promised to provide
the matter in question.   My father paid this sum ·
to the bookseller soon after he had attended the
remains of his departed friend to the grave.   The
manuscripts of Oldys, consisting of a few books
written in a small hand, and abundantly inter-
lined, remained long in my father's possession,
but by desire of Dr. Percy, afterwards Bishop of
Dromore, were submitted to his inspection,
through the medium of Dr. Monsey, who was
an intimate friend of Dr. Percy.   They continued
in Dr. Percy's hands some years.   He had known
Mr. Oldys in the early part of his life, and spoke
respectfully of his character.   The last volume of
Oldys's manuscripts that I ever saw, was at my
friend the late Mr. William Gifford's house, in James
Street, Westminster, while he was preparing a
new edition of the works of Shirley ; and I learned
from him that it was lent to him by Mr. Heber.
. . . . . . My friend Mr. D'Israeli is mistaken in
saying that on 'the death of Oldys, Dr. Kippis,
editor of the *Biographia Britannica*, looked over
the manuscripts.'   It was not until near thirty
years after the death of Oldys, that they were
submitted to his inspection, and at his recommendation were purchased by the late Mr. Cadell."*

---

* *Records of my Life*, pp. 28, 29.   For the searching
inquiries after the missing biographical manuscripts of
Oldys made by Mr. Isaac D'Israeli, see his *Curiosities of
Literature*, edit. 1823, iii. 476.

Oldys was the fortunate possessor of a large collection of Italian Provèrbs, entitled *Giardino di Recreatione*, in manuscript, by John Florio, the editor of a *Dictionarie in Italian and English*, containing commendatory verses prefixed by Matthew Gwinne, Samuel Daniel, and two other friends. This volume afterwards belonged to Sir Isaac Heard, from whom it passed to Mr. B. H. Bright, and was sold in the sale of his manuscripts, on June 18, 1844. (Hunter's *Illustrations of Shakspeare*, i. 275.)

Among other books enriched with notes by Oldys is that of *England's Parnassus*, 8vo, 1600. It was ˅ owing to his bibliographical erudition that the name of the compiler of these "Choysest Flowers" became known. Wood, misapprehending the information given by Phillips in his *Theatrum Poetarum*, 1675, designated Fitz-Geffry as the compiler; but Oldys had discovered in one or two copies that the initials R. A. to the dedicatory Sonnet to Sir Thomas Mounson were signed R. Allot. To the signature R. A. Oldys has added the following note : —

"Mr. Edmund Bolton, in his *Hypercritica*, mentions Robert Allott and Henry Constable as two good poets in his days. So I conclude upon the whole, that the said Robert Allott, the poet, was the Collector of this book. John Weever, in his little book of *Epigrams*, printed in 12mo, 1600 (or the year before), yet, I think, quoted in this work, has the following lines:—

'Ad Ro: Allot, and Chr: Middleton.
'Quick are your wits, sharp your conceits,
  Short and more sweet your lays;
  Quick, but no wit; sharp, no conceit,
  Short and less sweet my praise.'"

A censure passed upon *England's Parnassus* by Oldys, in his Preface to Hayward's *British Muse*, 1738, though tinctured with too much severity, is certainly not unfounded in its general reprehension. He shrewdly and sarcastically concludes that the book, "bad as it is, suggests one good

d

observation upon the use and advantage of such
collections, which is, that they may prove more
successful in preserving the best parts of some
authors, than their works themselves." Mr. Warton, however, considers the extracts as made "with
a degree of taste:" and Sir S. Egerton Brydges
as " very curious and valuable." The last mentioned remarks (*Cens. Liter.* ii. 318), that the state
of our knowledge on these subjects is materially
altered since the time of Oldys ; who, though his
bibliographical erudition was very eminent, could
add, that " most of the authors were now so obsolete, that not knowing what they wrote, we can
have no recourse to their works, if still extant." *

Oldys's annotated copy of *England's Parnassus*
passed into the hands of Thomas Warton, and
subsequently came into the possession of Colonel
Stanley, at whose sale in April and May, 1813
(lot 378), it was purchased by Mr. R. Triphook as
his own speculation for 13*l.* 13*s.*

The most valuable and curious work left by
Oldys is an annotated copy of Gerard Langbaine's
Account of the early Dramatick Poets, Oxford,
1691, 8vo. It has already been stated (*antè*,
p. xi), that the *first* copy of this work with his
notes had passed into the hands of Mr. Coxeter.
After Mr. Coxeter's death his books and manuscripts were purchased by Osborne, and were
offered for sale in 1748. The book in question,
No. 10,131 in Osborne's Catalogue for that year,
was purchased either by Theophilus Cibber, or by
some bookseller who afterwards put it into his
hands ; and from the notes of Oldys and Coxeter,
the principal part of the additional matter furnished by Cibber (or rather by Shiels) for the
Lives of the Poets, 5 vols. 12mo. 1753, was unques-
tionably derived. Mr. Coxeter's manuscripts are
mentioned in the title-page, to whom, therefore,

* Thomas Park, in the Preface to the reprint of *England's Parnassus*, 1815.

the exclusive credit of the work is assigned, but which really belongs as much, if not more, to Oldys.

Oldys purchased a *second* Langbaine in 1727, and continued to annotate it till the latest period of his life. This copy was purchased by Dr. Birch, who bequeathed it to the British Museum. It is not interleaved, but filled with notes written in the margins and between the lines in an extremely small hand. Birch granted the loan of it to Dr. Percy, Bishop of Dromore, who made a transcript of the notes into an interleaved copy of Langbaine in four vols. 8vo. It was from Bishop Percy's copy that Mr. Joseph Haslewood annotated his Langbaine. He says, " His Lordship was so kind as to favour me with the loan of this book, with a generous permission to make what use of it I might think proper ; and when he went to Ireland, he left it with Mr. Nichols, for the benefit of the new edition of *The Tatler*, *Spectator*, and *Guardian*, with Notes and Illustrations, to which work his Lordship was by his other valuable communications a very beneficial contributor."

George Steevens likewise made a transcript of Oldys's notes into a copy of Langbaine, which at the sale of his library in 1800, was purchased by Richardson the bookseller for 9*l.*, who resold it to Sir S. Egerton Brydges in the same year for fourteen guineas. At the sale of the Lee Priory library in 1834, it fell into the hands of Thorpe of Bedford-street, Covent Garden, from whom the late Dr. Bliss purchased it on Feb. 7, 1835, for nine guineas. It is now in the British Museum.

Malone, Isaac Reed, and the Rev. Rogers Ruding, also made transcripts of Oldys's notes. The Malone transcript is now at Oxford; but Ruding's has not been traced. In a cutting from one of Thorpe's catalogues, preserved by Dr. Bliss, it is stated to be in two volumes, the price 5*l.* 5*s.*; that Ruding transcribed them in 1784, and that his

additions are very numerous. In Heber's Catalogue (Pt. iv. No. 1215) is another copy of Langbaine, with many important additions by Oldys,
Steevens, and Reed. This was purchased by Rodd
for 4*l*. 4*s*. In 1845, Edward Vernon Utterson had
an interleaved Langbaine. What has become of it?
It is scarcely possible to take up any work on
the History of the Stage, or which treats of the
biographies of Dramatic Writers, without finding
these curious *collectanea* of Oldys quoted to illustrate some or other obscure point. "The Biogra-
graphical Memoirs I have inserted in *Censura
Literaria*," remarks Sir S. E. Brydges, "have been
principally drawn from the minute and intelligent
inquiries, and indefatigable labours of Oldys, preserved in the interleaved copy of Langbaine.
Many of them are curious, and though parts have
already been given to the public in the *Biographia
Dramatica*, yet as they are in the originals from
whence that work borrowed them, it became not
only amusing but useful to record them in their
own form and words."

In the British Museum (Addit. MS. 12,523) is
a manuscript volume, in Oldys's hand writing, of
miscellaneous extracts for a work with the following title: "The Patron; or a Portraiture of Patronage and Dependency, more especially as they
appear in their Domestick Light and Attitudes.
A Capital Piece drawn to the Life by the Hands
of several Eminent Masters in the great School of
Experience, and addressed to a Gentleman, who
upon the loss of Friends, was about to settle in a
great Family."

The subjoined catalogue of the books found in
Oldys's library at the time of his death, cannot
fail to interest every one curious in bibliography.

OLDYS'S LIBRARY AND MANUSCRIPT WORKS.*

The collection of books formed by this accurate and laborious antiquary, through whose exertions English literature and bibliography have been so essentially improved, was purchased by Thomas Davies, author of *The Life of Garrick*, and offered for sale in "A Catalogue of the Libraries of the late William Oldys, Esq. Norroy King-at-Arms (author of *The Life of Sir Walter Raleigh*); the Rev. Mr. Emms of Yarmouth, and Mr. Wm. Rush, which will begin to be sold on Monday, April 12 [1762], by Thomas Davies."

The trifling prices which were asked for some books that are now esteemed amongst the scarcest in the language, will amuse the bibliomaniac of the present day, who, if his wishes tend towards the collection of early literature, not so much on the score of its rarity as from its utility, will assuredly lament that he did not live at a period when his taste and desires could have been so readily gratified.

The charge for that invaluably illustrated copy of Langbaine † must astonish those who are acquainted with the large sums which have been required for transcripts only of those important additions to our dramatic biography.

227. Nicolson's Historical Libraries, with a great number of MS. additions, references, &c. by the late Wm. Oldys, very fair 2*l*. 2*s*. 1736. [Now in the British Museum.]

230. Fuller's Worthies of England, with MS. corrections, &c. by Mr. Oldys.‡ A price had originally been

---

* From Fry's *Bibliographical Memoranda*, 4to. Bristol, 1816, p. 33.

† Mr. Fry is not correct. The famed annotated Langbaine, purchased of Davies by Dr. Birch for one guinea, is the edition of 1691. It would appear, however, from lot 1511 of the above list, that Oldys had commenced annotating Gildon's edition of 1699.

‡ "This copy," says Mr. Fry, "was purchased at the

d 3

attached to this article, but is obliterated, apparently by
the publisher.*

268. Linschoten's Voyages to the East Indies, with a
great many cuts, black-letter, 12s. 6d.†

593. A Collection of scarce and valuable Old Plays,
most of them in small quarto, amounting in all to above
450, with a written catalogue [no price.]

705. Virgil, translated into Scottish Meter, by Gawin
Douglas. Black-letter, Lond. 1553. 5s.‡

717. Complaints, containing Sundry Poems of the
World's Vanity, by Ed. Spenser, the Author's own edition, 1591. 2s. 6d.

719. The Book which is called the Body of Polycye,
black-letter, very fair, 1521. 5s.

720. The Book of Falconrie and Hawking, with Cuts,
black-letter, 1611. The Noble Art of Hunting, with Cuts,
black-letter, 1611, very fair. 6s.

725. Cooper's Chronicle, black-letter, neat, 1560. 3s.

728. Milton's Paradise Lost, in Ten Books, first edition, very fair, 1669. 5s.

736. Whetstone's English Mirror, 1586. Crowley's
Answer to Powndes Six Reasons, 1581: black-letter. 3s.

738. Goulart's Admirable and Memorable History of
the Times, Englished by Grimeston, 1607. 2s.

832. Enemy to Unthryftiness, a perfect Mirrour for
Magistrates, by Whetstone, and six other Curious Tracts.
7s. 6d.

---

sale of George Steevens's library by the late Mr. Malone,
in whose collection it still remains." Mr. Isaac D'Israeli
states, however, that Steevens's copy contained a transcript of Oldys's notes. He says, "The late Mr. Boswell
showed me a Fuller [Worthies] in the Malone collection,
with Steevens's transcription of Oldys's notes, which
Malone purchased for 43l. at Steevens's sale; but where
is the original copy? " (Curiosities of Literature, Second
Series, iii. 469, ed. 1823.) In Steevens's Sale Catalogue
it is thus described: "Lot 1799. Fuller (Thos.) Worthies
of England, a very fine copy in russia, with the portrait
by Loggan, and Index; a most extraordinary and match-
less book, the late Mr. Steevens having bestowed uncommon pains in transcribing every addition to render it
valuable, written in his peculiarly neat manner, fol.
Lond. 1662."

* The price was 1l. 11s. 6d. — Bolton Corney.

† At the Roxburghe sale it fetched 10l. 15s.

‡ At the Roxburghe sale it fetched 7l. 7s.

836. Lavaterus of Ghosts and Spirits walking by Night; of atraunge Noises, Crackes, &c., black-letter, 1596. A Thousand Notable Things of Sundry Sortes, by Lupton; black-letter, no date, and three others. 6s.

852. Hyperius's Practica of Preaching, translated by Ludbam, blac'<-letter, 1577. Tragical History of the Troubles and Civill Warres of the Low Countries, black-letter, 1581. 4s.

1511. Lives and Characters of tha English Dramatick Poets, by Langbaine and Gildon, with MS. additions by Oldys, 1699. 3s. 6d.

1683. The British Librarian, six numbers in boards, 1738. 1s. 6d.

1684. The same, bound. 2s.

2449. A Manifest Detection of the most vyle and detestable Use of Dice Play, black-letter, sewed, 1552. 1s. 6d.

2450. Vaughan's Golden Grove, 1600. 1s.

2554. Wit and Drollery, 1682. 1s.

2569. Stevenson's Norfolk Drollery, 1673.* 1s.

2570. Shakespeare's Poems, 1640. 1s.

2572. Vilvain's Epitome of Essays, 1654. 1s. 6d.

2573. Collop's Poesie Reviv'd, 1656. 1s.

2574. Wit Restor'd, 1658. 1s. 6d.

2575. Wits' Recreation, 1640. 1s. †

2579. Palingenius's Zodiake of Life, Englished by Googe, black-letter, 1565. 2s. 6d.

2580. Dunton's Maggots, 1685. 1s. 6d.

2581. The Muses' Recreation, 1656. 1s.

2633. Lingua: or the Combat of the Tongue, 1657. 1s. 6d.

2634. Lilly's Six Court Comedies, 1632. 2s.

₊ The last twelve articles are in verse.

William Oldys's Manuscripts.

3612. Catalogue of Books and Pamphlets relating to the City of London, its Laws, Customs, Magistrates; its Diversions, Public Buildings; its Misfortunes, viz. Plagues, Fires, &c., and of every thing that has happened remarkable in London from 1521 to 1759, with some occasional remarks. Folio.‡

---

* About this period many books were published with a similar title, such as Songs of Love and Drollery, 1654; Bristol Drollery, 1656; Sportive Wit, or the Lusty Drollery, 1656; Holborn Drollery, 1672; Grammatical Drollery, 1682; all in verse. — *Fry.*

† Fetched at the Roxburghe sale, 4l. 8s.

‡ Gough (*British Topog.* ed 1780, i. 567) informs

Quarto.

3613. Of London Libraries; with Anecdotes of Collectors of Books, Remarks on Booksellers, and of the first publishers of Catalogues. [See *postea*, p. 58.]

3614. Epistolæ G. Morley ad Jan. Ulitium.

3615. Catalogue of graved Prints of our most eminent countrymen, belonging to Mr. Oldys.

3616. Orationes habitæ in N. C. 1655: English verses.

3617. Memoirs relating to the Family of Oldys. [In British Museum, Addit. MS. 4240.]

3618. Barcelona: or the Spanish Expedition under the Conduct of the Right Hon. the Earl of Peterborough; a Poem by Mr. Farquhar, never before published. [This seems to have been copied from the printed edition. — *Bolton Corney.*]

3619. The Life of Augustus, digested into fifty-nine Schemes, by James Robey.

Octavo et infra.

3620. The Apophthegms of the English Nation, containing above 500 memorable sayings of noted Persons, being a Collection of Extempore Wit, more copious than any hitherto published. [It was probably founded on a

---

us, that "he had been favoured by George Steevens, Esq., with the use of a thick folio of titles of books and pamphlets relative to London, and occasionally to Westminster and Middlesex, from 1521 to 1758, collected by the late Mr. Oldys; with many others added, as it seems in another hand. Among them are many purely historical, and many of too low a character to rank under the head of topography or history. The rest, which are very numerous, I have inserted marked O, with corrections, &c., of those I had myself collected. Mr. Steevens purchased this MS. of T. Davies, who bought Mr. Oldys's library. It had been in the hands of Dr. Berkenhout, who had a design of publishing an English Topographer, and may possibly have inserted the articles in a different hand. 5*l.* 5*s.* is the price in the first leaf. In a smaller MS. Mr. Oldys says he had inserted 360 articles in the folio, April 12, 1747, and that the late Alderman Billers had a fine collection of tracts, &c., relating to London." — "Mr. Oldys's collection of titles for London have passed from Mr. Steevens to Sir John Hawkins." (*Ib.* i. 761*.) Sir John Hawkins's library was destroyed by fire.

MS. collection of earlier date. — *Life of Sir Walter Raleigh.* — *Bolton Corney.*]

3621. Description of all Kinds of Fish.

3622. The British Arborist; being a Natural, Philological, Theological, Poetical, Mythological, Medicinal, and Mechanical History of Trees, principally native to this Island, with some Select Exoticks, &c. Not finished.

3623. Description of Trees, Plants, &c. [Addit. MS. 20,724.]

3624. Collection of Poems written above one hundred years since.

3625. Trinarchodia: the several Raignes of Richard II., Henry IV., and Henry V. in verse, supposed to be written 1650. [This volume became the property of J. P. Andrews: Park describes it, *Restituta,* iv. 166. — *Bolton Corney.*]

3626. Collection of Poems by Mr. Oldys.

3627. Mr. Oldys's Diary, containing several Observations relating to Books, Characters, &c. [Printed in this volume.]

3628. Collections of Observations and Notes on various subjects.

3629. Memorandum Book, containing as above.

3630. Table of Persons celebrated by the English Poets.

3631. Catalogue of MSS. written by Lord Clarendon.

3632. Names of English Writers, and Places of their Burial, &c.

3633. Description of Flowers, Plants, Roots, &c.

*3633. Description of all Kinds of Birds. [See Addit. MS. 20,725.]

" So end," says Mr. Fry, " the minutiæ of this curious Catalogue, which I have thought it not incurious to record, more especially as Mr. Dibdin, whilst noticing the interleaved Langbaine, in his *Bibliomania,* does not seem to have been aware of its passing through the hands of the humble friend of Dr. Johnson."

Gough (*British Topog.,* i. 31, ed. 1780) says, " I have seen a first volume of a translation of Camden's *Britannia,* in 2 vols. 4to. by W. O., Esq. [probably William Oldys], printed by R. Penny, in Wine Office Court, Fleet Street, but not dated." This work is now in the Bodleian library. See

Bandinel's *Catalogue of the Gough Collection,* p. 17.

Here we must terminate our notice of this distinguished writer and indefatigable antiquary, whose extended life was entirely devoted to literary pursuits, and whose copious and characteristic accounts of men and books, have endeared his memory to every lover of English literature. If Oldys possessed not the erudition of Johnson or of Maittaire, he had at least equal patience of investigation, soundness of judgment, and accuracy of criticism, with the most eminent of his contemporaries. One remarkable trait in his character was the entire absence of regard for literary and posthumous fame, whilst he never begrudged his labour or considered his toil unproductive, so long as his researches substantiated Truth, or promoted the study of the History of Literature, which in other words is the history of the mind of man. Hence the very sweepings of his library, as so much precious ore, have since been industriously collected, and enrich the works of Malone, Ritson, Reed, Douce, Brydges, and others, and will always serve, as it were, for landmarks to those following in his wake. In his own peculiar departments of literature — history and biography — he has literally exhausted all the ordinary sources of information; and when he lacked the opportunity to labour himself, or to fill up the circle of his knowledge, he has nevertheless pointed out to his successors new or unexplored mines, whence additional *facts* may be gleaned, and the object of his life — the development of Truth — be secured.

DIARY OF WILLIAM OLDYS, ESQ.

DIARY OF WILLIAM OLDYS, ESQ.

Norroy King-at-Arms.

1737, June 22. Mrs. Cooper came to my chambers: said she would return me Puttenham's *Art of Poesy*, Browne's *Pastorals*, and Sir Henry Wotton, when she had finished her extracts for the second volume of her *Muses' Library*[1] to be published by Christmas.

To keep the large old MS. volume of the statutes of the Order of the Garter with the Arms of the Knights thereof, their portraits and Illuminations of the Ceremonies of the Order of the Bath composed *temp.* Henry VII. and VIII., till Mr. V. [Vertue?] has seen it. To take particular notice of Talbot's Rose, a sheet printed from a copper-plate and bound in this book, entitled " The Union of the Roses of the Families of Lancaster and York, with the arms of those who have been chosen Knights

----

[1] " The Muses' Library, or a Series of English Poetry from the Saxons to the Reign of King Charles II. By Elizabeth Cooper. London, printed for T. Davies, 1738, 8vo." There are some copies of this work with the imprint " Printed for James Hodges, 1741," and others with " Vol. I." on the title and last leaf; but notwithstanding these variations, no more than one volume, or one edition, was ever printed. It is said to be mostly compiled by William Oldys. Mrs. Cooper died on the 5th August, 1761, five months after the death of Oldys.

B

of the Garter from that time to this day, 1589."
In this Rose the arms of all those who have been
(since the marriage in 1486 of King Henry VII.
of the House of Lancaster, which bore the Red
Rose, with Elizabeth, daughter of Edward IV. of
the House of York, whose ensign was the White
Rose) chosen into the Order of the Garter, insti-
tuted about 20 Edward III. are orderly set down.
The English arms placed within the Rose; those
of Foreign princes in the leaves beneath. There
are the heads of Henry VII. and his Queen Elizabeth engraved at the two upper corners over
this great crowned Rose, also in the flowery leaves
of it, the said King Henry, his son, King Henry
VIII., Queen Mary, and Queen Elizabeth, between the arms of the Knights Companion, who
have all their names and dates of their creations
subscribed. At the bottom Æg. Pluventor; sold
in the Black Friers, Tho. Talbot, composuit; Jo-
docus Hondius, Flander. Sculps. Londini, and
the date is 1589.[2]

June 29. Saw Mr. Ames's old MS. on vellum,
entitled *Le Romant de la Rose*, which cost forty
crowns of gold at Paris when first written, as appears by the inscription at the end.[3] It had been
Bishop Burnet's book, his arms being pasted in it;
and Mr. Rawlinson's, being mentioned in one of
his Catalogues. In the same Catalogue also is
mentioned Sir William Monson's collections[4], which
Mr. West bought and lent me before the fatal

---

[2] Noticed in Moule's *Bibliotheca Heraldica*, p. 36. In
the Cotton library (Vesp. D. xvii.) is "A miscellaneous
collection concerning Abbies and various historical matters, extracted from chronicles, rolls of noble families,
their pedigrees, &c. by Thomas Talbot."

[3] See Herbert's *Ames*, vol. i. p. xxxix.

[4] Sir William Monson, an Admiral of note in the reign
of James I., formed considerable collections, principally
relating to the affairs of the navy. There are occasional
copies from them, and allusions to them, in papers in the
State Paper Office.

fire happened at his chambers in the Temple, where
this probably was burnt, and near 3000*l.* worth
of other like most valuable curiosities.[5] Mr. Ames
also told me that the Society for Promoting of
Learning [6] intended to begin at last with publishing Sir Thomas Roe's Letters, but heard nothing
of the " Considerations " I wrote in six sheets,
above two years ago, *upon the best method for their
publication*, at the request of Samuel Burroughs,
Master in Chancery, who made me promises of
being concerned in the edition, and of other
favours for my furnishing him with many intel-
ligences and tracts, when he was writing his pamphlet about *Fines* [7]; but I never had any of those
favours, nor six of twenty-one volumes of tracts I
lent him ; nor the three Catalogues of my pamphlets, nor those " Considerations " in MS. which
I bestowed half a year upon, though I hear they are
in the hands of Richardson the printer.[8]   Mr.

---

5 This lamentable fire occurred on Jan. 4, 1737, when
upwards of twenty chambers were destroyed, containing
a large number of valuable books and manuscripts.
It is noticed by Hearne in his Preface to Leland's *Itinerary*,
vol. i. p. xvi., edit. 1745. Among those who were sufferers
by this calamity were Counsellor York, Mr. West, Mr.
Peters, Mr. Floyer, Mr. Blew the librarian, Counsellor
Collins, &c. Mr. James West was subsequently one of
the vice-presidents of the Society of Antiquaries. The
Catalogue of his library, digested by Samuel Paterson,
is one of the richest extant in literary curiosities.

6 The Society for the Encouragement of Learning commenced its brief existence on February 5, 1736-7. See
Nichols's *Literary Anecdotes, passim.* For a list of the
works printed under its patronage, see Bowyer's *Anecdotes*, and Kippis's *Biog. Britan.*, ii. 441.

7 Published under the pseudonym of Everard Fleetwood.

8 This manuscript is in the British Museum (Addit.
MS. 4168.), and is entitled " Some Considerations upon
the Publication of Sir Thomas Roe's Epistolary Collections." On a fly-leaf Samuel Richardson has added this
·note : " This was written (I think) by Mr. Oldys, and by
him tendered to Samuel Burroughs, Esq., as his senti-

Ames also told me that Mr. Cook is the author
of Seymour's *Survey of London*, in 2 vols. fol.
[1734.][9]

July 2, Saturday. Sent a letter to Mr. Anstis
about the Old MS. of Knights of the Garter and
Bath. He sent his son to see it when I was
abroad.

4, Monday. Returned Sir T. More's works :
some of his English poetry therein might be for
Mrs. Cooper's work, or Mr. Hayward's [*British
Muse*] on Fortune, &c.

7, Thursday. Saw Mr. Lockman.[10] Told me
he had finished the Life of Mr. Samuel Butler
for the *General Dictionary*. That he had had
much conversation with Mr. Longueville, who has
Butler's *History and Progress of Learning*[1] — a
poem by the same hand in Hudibrastick verse,
and other writings of his in prose never printed.
That he has also got an original picture of Butler,
painted by Lilly or Riley. That Butler had 300*l.*
for *Hudibras ;* that he died in Rose Street, Covent
Garden, and was 80 years of age.— Saw Dr. Pe-
pusche ;[2] to have farther talk about his rare old
musical collections.

----

ments about the Method of publishing Sir Thomas Roe's
Letters, &c." It comprises thirteen pages folio.

[9] This work has always been attributed, on the authority of Wm. Upcott, to John Mottley, the compiler of
Joe Miller's Jests ; but it would appear from the above,
that it was the compilation of Thomas Cooke, a dramatic
poet and miscellaneous writer, who died in great poverty
on Dec. 29, 1756. As Cooke was concerned with Mottley
in writing *Penelope*, a Dramatic Opera, 8vo., 1721, Seymour's *London* may have been their joint-production.

[10] Mr. John Lockman, Secretary to the British Herring
Fishery, a very honest man, but very indifferent poetas-
ter, best known for his share in the *General Dictionary*,
10 vols. fol. 1734-41. He died 2nd Feb. 1771.

[1] This, which is only a fragment, was printed (vol. i.
p 202.) in the edition of Butler's *Remains*, edited by
Thyer in 1759.

[2] John Christopher Pepusch, one of the greatest theo-

30. Old Mr. Booth[3], Treasurer of Gray's Inn, came to my chambers and very courteously brought me *Gervasii Tilberiensis de Necessariis Scaccarii Observantiis Dialogus.* 'Tis a very fair copy, in a thin folio bound in black calf, with a note of this Gervase of Tilbury, nephew to King Henry II. from John Bale in his *Scriptor. Illustrium Majoris Britanniæ Catalogo,* Cent. 3. fol. 250., written by Mr. W. Lambard the Antiquary in 1572, whose book this then was, as appears by his name, both at the beginning, in a kind of inscription to Sir Thomas Bromley, and the end of it. He has made short marginal observations throughout, and some corrections, having had the advantage of comparing it with a more antient copy, this not being older in all probability than King Henry the Eighth's time.[4] I take it to be the same book which Mr. Madox published not many years since of the Exchequer[5], and have a notion that Mr. Hearne published a copy of the black Book of the Exchequer.[6] There is in the last chapter but one [two] of the first part of this MS. copy, entitled *Quid liber Judiciarius, et ad quid compositus sit,* the best reason given for the meaning of Domesday Book, composed at the command

retic musicians. He was organist at the Charterhouse, and died 20th July, 1752, aged eighty-five. His curious library was dispersed after his death.

5 Oldys, in the *British Librarian,* pp. 286. 374., acknowledges the obligations he is under to Nathaniel Booth, Esq. for the use of his library. Mr. Booth was a bencher of Gray's Inn, and Controller of the Fines and Green Wax Money in the Court of Exchequer. He died *s. p.* Oct. 9, 1745, aged eighty-five.

4 Who is the present possessor of this MS.?

5 Madox's *History of the Exchequer* was first published in 1711, fol. Gervasius' *Ancient Dialogue* is appended to it.

6 Hearne published *Liber Niger Scaccarii, Wilhelmique etiam Worcestrii Annales Rerum Anglicarum.* Oxon. 1728, 8vo. 2 vols.

of William the Conqueror, that ever I met with, no ways favouring their conjecture who derive it from *Domus Dei*.[7] But why Sir Hen. Spelman in his *Glossary* fathers that chapter upon Henry de Blois, Bishop of Winchester, I know not, nor believe that Mr. Madox his reasons that the whole treatise was written by Richard Nigelli filius or Nelson, Bishop of London, will prevail with every body to disinherit old Gervase of Tilbury, who has been in possession so many years. Yet Selden, in *Titles of Honour*, is also for depriving old Gervase of it from the authorities there quoted.[8]

August 8. Rec[d] Mr. Ames's letter of thanks for the fine pictures I gave him drawn with a pen, &c., and desire from Mr. Ward, Professor of Rhetoric, at Gresham College, who is writing the history thereof, that I would furnish him with what I farther found of Edward Brerewood, which I gave him two days after when I returned his book of witches.

I went that night with him to his club, and saw the operations of the phosphorus, which the owner told me he made of nothing but flour and allum.

---

[7] The passage, as given in a translation by W. B., Gent., in Lansdowne MS. 610. p. 30[b]., is as follows: "This booke is by the countrymen called Doomesday Booke, that is, the Day of Judgment by a metaphor. For as the judgment of the strict and dreadful accompt of the last day can by noe act or evasion be eluded; soe when there is any controversie in the kingdome which are there recorded, when they come to the Booke, noe man may denye or decline the judgment thereof without punishment. For this cause we call the same Booke, 'The Booke of Judgment'; not because certaine doubts are there determined, but because from that, as from the Day of Judgment, there lyes noe appeale."

[8] Professor Liebrecht, the learned Editor of *Des Gervasius von Tilbury Otia Imperialia. In Einer Auswahl neu herausgegeben*, Hanover, 1856, shares, however, the opinion of Madox, that this Treatise on the Exchequer was written by Richard Bishop of London, and not by Gervase.

Invited by Dr. Harris to his brother's [9] at Hummerton, near Hackney, where old Mr. Strype, author of many voluminous pieces of ecclesiastical history is still alive [10] and has the remainder of his once rich collection of MS. tracts, &c.

Aug. 13. Rec[d] letter from Mrs. Cooper to borrow old Marlow's poem of *Hero and Leander* for the continuation of her *Muses Library*; sent by the servant a very scarce collection of old poetry, called *The Paradise of Dainty Devices* [1], in which are several pieces written by the old Lord Vaux in King Henry the Eighth's time, the Earl of Oxford, Sir W. Raleigh, Mr. Edwards, Jasper Haywood, Hunnis, Churchyard, Kinwelmersh, Lloyd, Whetstone, &c., printed 4°. 1578. To borrow one of Caxton's books of Sir Hans Sloane, and remember to apply the story of Absyrtus in the preface for Mr. Hayward's Collection of select thoughts from our old poets.

---

[9] Mr. Harris, an Apothecary at Homerton, married to a grand-daughter of Strype, and in whose house Strype died.

[10] An interesting picture of Strype in his old age is given by Dr. Knight in a letter to Zachary Grey, dated 24 March, 1733-4, printed in Nichols's *Literary Anecdotes*, v. 360.:—" I made a visit to old Father Strype when in town last: he is turned ninety, yet very brisk, and with only a decay of sight and memory; he would fain have induced me to undertake Archbishop Bancroft's Life; but I have not stomach to it, having no great opinion of him on more accounts than one. He had a greater inveteracy against the Puritans than any of his predecessors. Mr. Strype told me that he had great materials towards the life of the old Lord Burleigh and Mr. Foxe, the Martyrologist, which he wished he could have finished, but most of his papers are in characters; his grandson is learning to decypher them." Strype died on the 13th December, 1737—a few months only after Oldys's visit to him.

[1] *The Paradise of Dainty Devices*, first published in 4to. 1576, and reprinted in Brydges's *British Bibliographer.*

To enquire at Covent Garden Coffee House
who bought Sir Walter Ralegh's Head, said to be
painted by Zucchero ; Beaumont and Fletcher by
Cornelius Johnson [Jansen] ; Ben Johnson, and
Spenser, and Shakespear, by Mittens [John ?]
Greenhill the painter ; and Cowley by Sir Peter
Lely ; Secretary Thurloe by Dobson ; and Congreve on copper by Sir Godfrey Kneller, as is
pretended in the catalogue for the sale of Pictures
there, on the 10th of March last.

Aug. 25. Rec[d] of Purser, the printer in Bartholomew Close, the first sheet of Mr. Hayward's
British Muse, and a proof of the second, and promise to send me every sheet as soon as composed
to correct, and a fair sheet as soon as wrought off,
that I may make timely observations for the Preface.   Mr. Booth brought me two MSS. to make
use of: the one a Declaration of the Hardships of
John Danyell of Deresbury, Esq. in the fine of
3000*l.*, loss of his estate worth 20,000*l.*, and im-
prisonment which he endured upon account of the
Earl of Essex; 'tis the original in 4to., dated at the
end of the Preface from the Fleet in 1602, but he
has several things in it written below Queen Elizabeth's reign, as letters, petitions, &c., to King
James, Lord Chancellor Egerton, &c., ending with
Danyell's Disasters, a narrative of his said
Hardships.[2]   The other MS. is a miscellany, beginning with a letter of Sir Francis Walsingham
to the Earl of Pembroke, and some of the Earl of

---

[2] John Danyell, of Deresbury, was Ward to the Queen:
ob. 1609.   In the State Paper Office, Domestic James I.
vol. lii. 33., is a "License to John and Jane Danyell, to
print and publish the works entitled 'Danyell's Disasters:' 'The varyable accidents in a private man's lyffe;'
and 'A Declaration of the fatal accidents of Jane Danyell.'"   For some particulars of John Danyell's venality,
consult Camden's *Annals of Queen Elizabeth*, fol. 1688.
p. 630., and Kippis's *Biog. Britan.*, art. PETER BALES, i.
543., from the pen of William Oldys.

Leycester's letters from the Low Country, particularly one about the death of Sir Philip Sidney, written to Sir Thos. Hennage, 23 Sept. 1586 ; A Speech about the Queen of Scots ; Her answer to Mons' de Salant ; The Book of the whole Navy (Royal) ; An analogy or resemblance between Joan Queen of Naples, and Mary Queen of Scots, with the addition and precedents or examples of Emperors and Popes, &c., putting other princes to death ; A letter from Sir Edward Stanley ; *Liber Pacis* or *Nomin: Justiciar: ad Assiss: in Com: subscript.* ; Number and names of all the ships, &c., appertaining to the River of Chester, by W. Wale, Maior, at the command of the Earl of Derby, Lord-Lieutenant of Lancashire and Cheshire, 1585 ; A. Cosbye's letter to Sir W. Stanley from Utricht, about surrendering the town of Deventer ; Number of serviceable men and munition in the Isle of Man ; A particular valuation of Guddischen Demain ; The strange apparition of Death, Famine, and Pestilence in France, April 18, 1587 ; A letter of the Earl of Leicester from Dort, 22nd Aug. 1587 ; Arthur Aly from the Hague, 15 Oct. 1587, to Rt. Hon. Mr. Jno. Woolley of the Privy Council ; Answers of Christopher Southworth, priest, to interrogatories ; The Earl of Leycester to Mr. Woolley, 3rd Oct. 1587 ; again to him, 9th Oct. following ; The whole yearly revenue of the Kingdom of Spain ; The confession of Edward Burnell, Jan. 1, 1586 ; His examination before Sir George Carey and Ralph Lane, Esq., same day ; The manner of the execution of the Queen of Scots, 8th of Feb., in the presence of such whose names are underwritten ; A prophesy signed Merlin applied to Sir Francis Drake ; Sir Walter Ralegh's five preferments about the year 1586 or 87 ; A sonnet of Sir Walter Ralegh's, one stanza and distich of which was printed in the old *Art of English Poesie*, 4to. 1589, which I have quoted in his Life ; A particu-

lar of some new year's gifts, beginning with my
cousin Katherine Howard's new year's gift, &c.,
with several other things up and down the book
relating to some Estates, &c., of Henry Earl of
Derby, which makes me think the collection was
made by him or somebody nearly under him.

Aug. 28. Mr. Vertue called upon me, and we
appointed to go next Sunday to Mr. Ames. Told
me he had been at Penshurst, the Lord Leicester's,
again; took a copy of Sir Philip Sidney's picture,
and that he saw in the library Sir Philip's Apology for, or Defence of, his Uncle Robert Earl of
Leicester, written with his own hand in five or
six sheets of paper, in answer to some libel then
written or published against him, which I imagine
to have been Father Parsons his green coat, afterwards called *Leicester's Commonwealth*, 4° and 8°,
1541; and he observed that the said defence or
apology ends with Sir Philip's challenge to main-
tain with his sword what he had herein asserted
with his pen against the said author of the said
libell, if he was a gentleman, in any part of the
world.[3]

Aug. 29. Dined with Mr. Ames; saw his collection of old Title-pages, and Mr. Lewis his intended
Title-page for his *Life of Maister William Caxton*[4],
our first printer, which I could in very few of the
particulars approve of; it being too circumstantial,
and giving us most of the private history of the man
in the first page of the book. Besides, the sub-
joining a poetical motto in French, from a modern
French poet, and that a translation rather on the
art of writing than printing, is too great an im-

---

[3] Sir Philip Sydney's Defence of his Uncle is printed in
Colline's *Letters and Memorials of State*, fol. 1746, vol. i.
pp. 61-68.
[4] " Life of Mayster Wyllyam Caxton, of the Weald of
Kent, the first Printer in England." By the Rev. John
Lewis, of Margate. Lond. 1737, royal 8vo. 150 copies
were printed with a fictitious portrait of Caxton.

propriety, too foreign, noways honouring his
worthy or his work, nor becoming the course and
character of an antiquary. Therefore, I recommended rather one from Mrs. Weston's Latin poem
of typography.[5] Supped with Mr. Thompson [6] at
St. Saviour's, and borrow'd his Caxton's *Tully de
Senectute* for the fifth number of *The British Librarian*; was witness to his paying a legacy to
Hasselden of 30*l.* Sent a letter to Mr. Ames
about the title of Mr. Lewis's *Life of Caxton*, and
about the twenty hundred weight of waste books,
at 25*s.* per cwt. Wrote an answer to Mr. Anstis
at Mortlake about the MS. collections, relating to

---

[5] Elizabeth Joanna Weston, a learned lady of the six-
teenth century. The poem is printed in her *Opuscula*,
8vo. 1724, p. 147.

[6] Sir Peter Thompson, Knt. was the third son of Capt.
Thomas Thompson, of Poole, co. Dorset, in which town
Sir Peter was born Oct. 30, 1698. Sir Peter was engaged
in mercantile pursuits more than forty years, during
which period he chiefly resided in Mill Street, Bermond-
sey.   He was elected F.S.A. 1743; appointed high-
sheriff for Surrey, 1745; and represented the borough of
St. Albans in parliament from 1747 to 1754. In 1763, he
withdrew from commercial affairs to enjoy the pleasures
of studious retirement. He died on October 30, 1770.
His valuable library and museum became the property
of his kinsman Peter Thompson, who in 1782 was a captain of the company of grenadiers in the Surrey militia.
Sir Peter collected, at great expence, all the antient records that could be found relating to the town of Poole,
which he liberally communicated to Mr. Hutchins for his
History of Dorsetshire. His materials for the Life of
Joseph Ames were used by Mr. Gough in the Memoirs
prefixed to Mr. Herbert's edition of the *Typographical
Antiquities.*   Mr. Oldys, in the *British Librarian,* acknowledges his obligations to "his ingenious friend Mr.
Peter Thompson, for the use of several printed books,
which are more scarce than manuscripts; particularly
some, set forth by our first printer in England; and
others, which will rise, among the curious, in value, as,
by the depredations of accidents or ignorance, they decrease in number."—Nichols's *Lit. Anecdotes,* v. 258. 511.

the Order of the Garter, which he thinks is the
same book with that he formerly borrowed of a
noble peer, with the arms of Mr. Ashmole upon
it, and which had been missing some time out of
the said nobleman's library, whom he promises
shall make a recompence suitable to what it cost,
if it be his, and is restored to him ; further desir-
ing direction how to behave himself to discover
the person who took it away.

Sep. 1. Saw Mr. Wm. Jones's [7] curious library,
and fine collection of shells, fossils, &c., at his
house next the Salt Office, in York Buildings.

2. Sent another letter to Mr. Anstis, accepting
his invitation to Mortlake, promising to be with
him next Wednesday. Mr. Booth, when he called
yesterday, said he had manuscripts enough to
supply several *British Librarians*, and that he
would bring me the old Record relating, as I remember, to the Forest of Delamere, when Mr.
Holmes of the Tower had transcribed it.

4. Dined with Mr. Vertue, and went with him
to Mr. Ames in the afternoon. Returned Mr.

---

[7] Father of Sir William Jones.

[8] George Holmes, Keeper of the Records in the Tower
of London : born in 1662, and died 16th Feb. 1748-9.
His curious collection of books, prints, and coins were
sold by auction in 1749.

[9] Joseph Ames, Secretary of the Society of Antiquaries,
was originally a ship-chandler in Wapping. Late in life
he took to the study of antiquities ; and besides his *Typographical Antiquities*, 4to. 1749, he published a *Catalogue of English Heads*, 8vo. 1748, being the first attempt
at giving a list of portraits, since followed up by Granger, Noble, Bromley, Walpole, &c. He died in 1759. His
library and prints were sold by auction in the following
year. Oldys, in his *British Librarian*, acknowledges his
obligations to Mr Ames, whom he styles " a worthy preserver of antiquities," and returns him many thanks "for
the use of one ancient relique of the famous Wicliffe."
This was an illuminated MS. on vellum, called " Wicliffe's
Pore Caitiff."

Thompson's Caxton, and borrowed Sir Thomas
Elyot's *Governour*.[10]

6. Mr. Vertue shewed me two curious limnings
by old Isaac Oliver and his son Peter.[1] The first
was of Sir Philip Sidney, in a small oval in a blue
ground. His hair light brown, pretty full and
dark shaded; his face pale or somewhat wan, perhaps the colours only somewhat faded; his eyes
gray, very lively and sharp; his nose gently rising; his beard thin; his dress a falling laced
band, with a scollop edging; his vest, or doublet,
white sattin corded, and laid along crossways very
thickly with silver-lace, with this mark on the
right hand Φ.[2] The other, by Peter Oliver, is of
Sir Edward Harley, Knight of the Bath, grandfather to the Earl of Oxford. 'Tis somewhat
larger than the other, set in gold, painted on a
brown ground, as I remember, black short hair,
roundish face, black eyes, picked beard; dressed
in a ruff, close jacket or doublet, blue or greyish
coloured, and flowered with black, and a red rib-
bon about his neck. This motto to the right, *Ter
et amplius*, and this mark to the left, PO, both in
gold letters. They are both delicate pieces, but
the former has the hair more finely laboured, and
the skin more tenderly stippled. The latter is
freer, bolder, fresher. Mr. Vertue is graving

---

[10] This work is noticed by Oldys in *The British Li-
brarian*, p. 261. It is entitled "The Boke named the
GOVERNOUR; devised by Sir Thomas Elyot, Knyght.
Imprinted at London, in Flete-strete, in the House of
Tbos. Berthelet, *cum privilegio ad imprimendum solum*,"
8vo. 1553: 216 leaves, besides Tables, &c.

[1] *Vide* Walpole's *Anecdotes of Painting*, ed. 1849, i.
176. 221., for notices of these two miniature painters.

[2] The celebrated work of Isaac Oliver, formerly at
Cowdray, had this same mark. It was a picture of three
sons of Viscount Montague. (Walpole, *Ancc.*, ed. Dallaway, i. 297.) A miniature of Sir Philip Sydney by the
same artist was purchased by Horace Walpole at West's
sale for 16*l.* 5*s.* (*Ibid.* 299.)

C

them both: one for the publick, the other for the
Earl of Oxford. He shewed me several other miniatures, many of them his own painting. His
Queen of Scots, a full-length, seems to have most
engaged his pains; and his miniature of Sir Walter Ralegh, in the silver armour, has a nearer ap-
proach to the beauty of the original than his
print before my Life of him, which makes the
face longer, and less graceful.

7. Dined with Mr. Anstis at his seat near Mortlake. Saw the Duke of Montague's letter to him,
by which it appears the old heraldical manuscript
before-mentioned was his Grace's, and that the
gentleman lately dead, a Mr. Grimes, among
whose books it was bought, had borrowed it of
him. It was the handwriting of Sir Thomas
Wriothesley, who died about 26 Henry VIII., in
which the statutes of the Order appear at the beginning of that book, who signs at the end his ini-
tial letters, Th.Wr. A. R. Greck, that is, Grekelade.[3]
All the old illuminations of the Order of the Bath
were graved in small compartments in one sheet
in Sir Edward Bysse's Upton *De Studio militari*
[fol. 1654]. And the Duke has graved the portraits at length of the old Earls of Salisbury, &c.,
in this book, which, with some others from other
illuminations, make up seventeen plates; and Mr.
Anstis has copied much of the arms and badges,
&c., of the Knights of the Garter in it, so that the
book has now been almost totally ransacked. Saw
several curious books, &c., in his library, and his
own book of the Order of the Garter, with many
manuscript additions interleaved, and written on

---

[3] Oldys has also the following notice of this manuscript
in his article FASTOLFF in the *Biographia Britannica*, ii.
1909: "Sir Thomas Wriothesley's Heraldical Collections
of the Knights of the Garter, Bath, &c., adorned with
their portraits, arms, &c., fol. MS. in the possession of the
late Duke of Montagu. See an abstract of this volume in
The British Librarian, p. 323."

the margins. Some talk with Mr. Haslin about the *Librarian*, and his taste is for only old things, and collating editions, distinguishing omissions, alterations, &c.; but I made an objection they could not except against about Dr. Drake's edition of Archbishop Parker's *Lives of the Archbishops*, wherein is received all the author's rejections, for which indiscrete labour he could con the said editor no thanks. Saw the pictures of Robert Earl of Leicester in a close reddish doublet, half-length, and his brother Ambrose, Earl of Warwick, in the dining-room. Heard that the Yelverton library now is in the possession of the Earl of Sussex [4], wherein are many volumes of Sir Francis Walsingham's State Papers.

23. Dr. Pepusch offer'd me any intelligence or assistance from his antient collections of musick, for a history of that art and its professors in England [5]

4 The Yelverton MSS. were all given by the Earl of Sussex to Lord Calthorpe, whose mother was of the Yelverton family, and at his death had not been opened, (Gough MS. quoted in Nichols's *Lit. Anec.* iii. 622.) A catalogue of them is printed in the *Cat. Manuscriptorum Angliæ et Hiberniæ*, tom. ii., part. i., pp. 113—174.

5 If Oldys made any collections for a History of Music, they were most probably handed over to Sir John Hawkins. David Erskine Baker, Hawkins, and Oldys, were at this time the leading writers in *The Universal Spectator*. Our musical knight appears to have been somewhat reluctant in acknowledging his obligations to his friends. Oldys, writing to Sir John Hawkins, reminds him that "the few materials I, long since, with much search, gathered up concerning Izaak Walton, you have seen, and extracted, I hope, what you found necessary for the purpose I intended them." But on turning to Sir John's *Life* of Walton, the reader will find but a scant acknowledgment for only one statement made by him, respecting some letters of Walton in the Ashmolean Museum. This throws some light on a passage in Grose's *Olio*, p. 139., where he tells us, that "among Oldys's works is a *Preface* to Izaak Walton's *Angling*." The edition of Walton's *Complete Angler*, 1760, contains an interesting biography of Charles Cotton from the pen

C 2

27. Mr. Coxeter told me that the Queen's [6] collection of Plays were offered by Mr. Cooke [7], who
first collected them, for fourscore guineas, and
were, as his, thought too dear; but after Mrs.
Oldfield [8] the actress died, and they were reported
to be her collection, then the Queen would have
them at any rate; and was reported, I think, in
the newspapers to have given 200*l.* for them; but,
as he tells me, she had them for six score guineas.
And it is not improbable but that volume of
ten of Massinger's *Plays*, which was about three
or four months since sold by Cock the auctioneer
(in the sale of Sclater Bacon's Books [9]), to the
Countess of Pomfret's footman for 3*l.* 10*s.* [10], was
bought to add to that collection. He also said
that Weaver [11], the dancing-master's collection of
plays, was more complete, which sold to Chitty the
merchant for 18*l.*, and that Sir Thomas Hanmer is
preparing an edition of Shakspeare.

Oct. 5. Received the last sheet of the first vo-

of William Oldys, making forty-eight pages, but abridged
in the later editions. The whole of this biographical
sketch has been used by Sir Harris Nicolas in his admirable Life of Charles Cotton, but the name of Oldys is
not once mentioned! Dr. Towers, who compiled the Life
of Cotton for Kippis's *Biog. Britannica*, has erroneously
attributed Oldys's Life of this Piscator and Poet to Sir
John Hawkins.

6 Caroline, Queen Consort of George II. Ob. Nov. 20,
1737.

7 Thomas Cooke, dramatist and miscellaneous writer.

8 Mrs. Oldfield died on Oct. 23, 1730. Her collection
of English Plays, in 218 volumes, was sold in 1731.

9 Thomas Sclater Bacon, whose library was sold on
March 14, and following days, 1736-7.

10 These ten plays by Massinger, 4to. (lot 720), sold for
3*l.* 16*s.* Their rarity is noticed by Oldys in his Preface
to Hayward's *British Muse*, p. xxii.

11 The name of John Weaver, that little dapper cheer-
ful man, is not to be found in any biographical dictionary.
He was buried in St. Chad's church, Shrewsbury, on
28th Sept. 1760. *Vide* " N. & Q.," 2nd Ser. iii. 89. 138.
297.

lume of Mr. Hayward's *British Muse*; with him heard at his house the account of Austin, the ink powder man, noted for his fireworks; also the great pudding he made for his customers; but more especially the pudding which about twelve or thirteen years since he baked ten feet deep in the Thames near Rotherhithe for a wager, by enclosing it in a great tin pan, and that in a great sack of lime; and after in about two hours and a half it was taken up, and eaten with much liking, being only a little overbaked. There was above an 100*l.* won upon this experiment.

Dec. 22. Went in the evening to see Mr. Nickolls near Queen Hythe, and he shewed me his collection of *Original Letters and Addresses to Oliver Cromwell,* all pasted into a large volume, folio; in number about 130, and written to him while he was Lieutenant of Ireland, General of the army in Scotland, and Protector of England, from the year 1650 to 1654 the greatest part, but some down to 1658, ending with an address to Richard Cromwell, and a Commission signed by Prince Rupert. They had been the collection of Mr. John Milton, and were preserved by Thomas Elwood the Quaker, who had been his amanuensis, from whom they descended to the master with whom Mr. Nickolls served his time, and so they came to him.[1] He says he has suffered half a

---

[1] These letters have since been printed, entitled, "Original Letters and Papers of State, addressed to Oliver Cromwell, concerning the Affairs of Great Britain, from the Year 1649 to 1658, found among the Political Collections of Mr. John Milton; now first published from the Originals, by John Nickolls, F.R. and A.S.S. fol. 1743." The originals of these Letters were long treasured up by Milton; from whom they came into the possession of Thomas Elwood. From Elwood they came to Joseph Wyeth, a merchant of London; from whose widow they were obtained by Mr. Nickolls, and eventually presented to the Society of Antiquaries. Mr. Nickolls was a Quaker, and his place of business as a mealman was

dozen or half a score of them to be made use of by Mr. Birch in his Life of Oliver Cromwell inserted in the *General Dictionary;* and it is certain if those other letters, written by Oliver Cromwell himself, which are still in being, as Mr. Ames tells me, in Sir Hans Sloane's possession, and in Ashmole's Museum at Oxford, through the gift of Dr. Massey, they would give a more perfect idea of the man and his actions than all that has been ·said of him by the particular writers of his Life, as the author of *Parallelum Olivæ* [fol. 1656.], S. Carrington, 8vo. 1659, H. Dawbeny, James Heath, Slingsby Bethel, J. Shirley, Le Sieur du Galardi, Gregorio Leti, L'Abbee Raguenet, and Mr. Kimber, or what all the general historians have written of him put together.

Jan. 25, 1737·8. Mr. Twells [2] goes out of town.

Feb. 20. At the sale of Mr. Sclater Bacon's library in the Piazza [Covent´Garden], there arose one book called the *Pastyme of People,* a thin fol. volume, with wooden cuts of the English kings, from William the Conqueror to the slaughter of King Richard III., written the 21st of Hen. VIII. or 1530, and soon after printed. And nobody then present, of near thirty gentlemen and booksellers, &c., had discovered it to be John Rastell's *Chronicles* but myself, wherefore it stopped at ten shillings, the extent of Mr. West's commission to Noorthouck, the bookseller, for it ; who, had he known what it was, would have raised it to 20*l.*, or he would have had it. But having apprised Mr. Ames of it, he got for the former sum

in Trinity parish, near Queenhithe. He was a curious collector of antiquities, and chosen F.S.A. Jan. 17, 1740: ob. Jan. 11, 1745. — Nichols's *Literary Anecdotes*, ii. 159.

[2] The Rev. Leonard Twells, M.A., Rector of the united parishes of St. Matthew, Friday Street, and St. Peter, Cheapside. At this time he was engaged on his great

one of the scarcest books in England.[3] Two [five] nights after he bought at the same place Caxton's *Game of Chesse*, the second edition, with wooden cuts, with his *Mirror of the World*, and Chaucer's translation, *Boetius de Consolatione Philosophie*, printed together by him in a thick folio about 1480 for two guineas.[4]

March 1. Mr. Thompson bought at Bacon's auction a book called, and often mistaken for, Caxton's Chronicle, but is indeed *The Chronicle of St. Albans*, compiled by one sometime schoolmaster in that town, printed 1483, for 3*l*. 4*s*.[5] Also another edition by Wynken de Worde, having the account of the Popes left out, and the Description of England, Wales, and Ireland added from the *Polychronicon*, fol. 1502. Also, another edition of this last book by Julian Notary, 1515.

3. Went to Leicester Square with Mr. Ames, and saw Mr. Vertue there, and had some discourse about his grand design of an Ichnographical Survey, or Map of London and all the suburbs; but Mr. Rocque and he are not yet come to an agreement.[6]

5. Dined at Mr. Thompson's, and took an extract of what his authors afforded of the writers on the antiquities of Essex. Dr. Oxley told me that Mr. Haynes was going on with Cecil's Letters[7], that he had two or three transcribers at

---

work, *The Theological Works of Dr. Pocock*, 2 vols. fol. 1740. He died 19th Feb. 1741-2.

[3] Lot 1464. The Pasthyme of People, fol. No date, sold for 11*s*.

[4] Lot 1614. Caxton's Boetius alone in Thorpe's Catalogue of 1849 is marked 105*l*. See " N. & Q.," 1ˢᵗ S. i. 126.

[5] Qy. Lot 1585, which sold for 8*l*. 1*s*. For a notice of this copy, see Nichols's *Literary Illustrations*, iv. 166.

[6] John Rocque's Survey of London, Westminster, and Southwark, 1746, 1751.

[7] *Collection of State Papers*, edited by Samuel Haynes and Wm. Murdin. Lond. 1740-59, 2 vols. folio.

work: intended to publish a volume at a time,
and gives hopes that Sir Walter Ralegh's will be
published among them. Mr. Smith shewed me
some good specimens of his art in reviving the
illuminated letters in old MSS., and intimated that
the Countess of Pomfret is very skilful in this work.

Mr. Ames called at Chambers. Thanked him
for his ancient Greek inscription of Crato; tells
me he had given Mr. Ward my last communications for his *History of Gresham College,*
about the time of knighting the Greshams. Informed him of a picture of Sir Thomas Gresham's at the old Countess of Oxford's sale. They
are to come and see it; and Mr. Thompson to see
the old record of Caxton's death and burial at
St. Margaret's, Westminster, for the use of Mr.
Lewis, whose Life of that our first printer is
in the press. Received the bookseller's title (in
a proof) of Mr. Hayward's *British Muse,* which I
noways like; and the abridgement they have procured of my Preface to it by a hasty hand, ignorant of the subject, and who has ungratefully left
out the acknowledgments which the author expressly desired I would make of those communications which have much enriched his said collection from our own poets.[8]

---

[8] *The British Muse,* by Thomas Hayward, 3 vols. 12mo.
Lond. 1738. In Oldys's annotated Langbaine, he thus
complains of the publisher's cupidity: "To this book I
wrote the Introduction, but the penurious publishers (to
contract it within a sheet), left out a third part of the
best matter in it, and made more faults than there were
in the original." Poor Oldys appears most sensibly to
have lamented the loss of this elaborate Dissertation on
the previous Collections of English poetry. In his own
copy of *The British Muse* (afterwards Thomas Warton's,
and latterly Mr. Douce's), he has thus expressed himself:
"In my historical and critical review of all the collections of this kind, it would have made a sheet and a half
or two sheets; but they for sordid gain, and to save a
little expense in print and paper, got Mr. John Campbell

8. Now I have found the author of Mr. Booth's
fine MS. in *Defence of the Lawful Regiment of
Women,* to have been Henry Earl of Northampton
himself; and he had this beautiful copy of it
made in the year 1613, which he then presented to
Sir Robert Cotton, to be preserved in his library.
The Dedication to Queen Elizabeth consists of
fifty pages. The rest of the book, 426 pages more
in folio, appears to have been written in the 32nd
year of her reign, or A.D. 1590. Mr. Booth told
me he bought the MS. in Chester. See A. Wood's
Athen. Oxon., Fasti, i. 102., edit. 1721 (Bliss's edit.
Fasti, i. 182.)[9]

Mar. 16. Mr. Joseph Morgan's *Life and Character of Prince Henry,* published from Sir Charles
Cornwallis and several other historians, dedicated
to the Prince of Wales, in which I find myself
mentioned with commendation for the *Life of Sir
Walter Ralegh* [10]; so that now there have been

---

to cross it and cramp it, and play the devil with it, till
they squeezed it into less compass than a sheet." According to Warton, this work is the most comprehensive
and exact common-place book of our most eminent
poets, throughout the reign of Queen Elizabeth and
afterwards.

9 Walpole (*Royal and Noble Authors,* i. 177., ed. 1759),
in his Life of the Earl of Northampton, mentions a MS.
of this work as being then in his possession, and another in
the Bodleian [Arch. A. 170.] In Harl. MS. 7021, art. 11,
occurs, " An Answere to the Coppie of a rayleinge Invec-
tive against the Regement of Woemen in generall, with
certaine maliparte Exceptions to divers and sundry Matters of State; written unto Queene Elizabeth by the
Right Honourable Henry Lord Howard, late Earle of
Northampton." 116 pages, fairly written.

10 The work alluded to by Oldys is entitled *The Life
and Character of Henry-Frederic, Prince of Wales,* written by Sir Charles Cornwallis, sometime Treasurer of His
Royal Highness's Household. The Dedication is signed
J. M. Lond. 8vo. 1738. At pp. 43, 44., Mr. Oldys is
commended as "a very exact and faithful writer," and
"an accurate biographer."

the following encomiums written concerning the
same in manuscript and print.

Letter from the Earl of Oxford, dated April
19, 1734 : —

" SIR,—

" By this day's post I received the enclosed
letter and paper from the Rev. Mr. Baker, of
St. John's College. You will let me know if you
would have me write to him again for any more
papers relating to Sir Walter Ralegh, as he mentions, and I will.   I am, your humble servant,

" OXFORD.

" P.S. You see that I take care to get you all
the information I can that you may depend on." [1]

Extract of another letter written by the said
Earl, and dated 10 Dec. 1734 : —

" You see I omitt no opportunity to furnish you
with every thing I can possibly towards the perfect-
ing the good work you have undertaken, and indeed
you deserve all encouragement, for you take true
pains."

In the *Literary Magazine*, 8vo. for January,
1736, there is an abstract of this Life introduced
with these words : " It is the duty of a biographer
to be industrious in collecting his materials, care-
ful in his choice of them, and regular in digesting
them.   Mr. Oldys has failed in neither of these
particulars.   He has taken in all the assistance
that could be had from printed books and manuscripts of the best credit.   He has been indefati-

---

[1] The kindness of this noble Earl is also thus acknow-
ledged by Oldys in his *Life of Sir Walter Ralegh, Works*,
ed. 1829, i. 62.: " The three letters, whereof 1 have here
given the substance in Ralegh's own words, were communicated to me by the Right Hon. the Earl of Oxford
[Edward, the second Earl], from the collections of the
reverend and learned Mr. Baker of St. John's College,
Cambridge, who copied them out of the originals."

gable in the search of authorities, and made a
proper and judicious use of whatever publick records or private anecdotes could afford for his
purpose."

Extract of a letter from Scarborough, by Rob[t]
Robinson, Esq., Recorder, dated 10th October,
1736 ; no consequence no more than the quotation
from Mrs. Elizabeth Cooper in her *Muses' Library*,
8vo. 1737, in her character of Sir Walter Ralegh.
A letter from Mr. George Vertue to me, dated
October 13, 1743, sent with Geo. Gascoigne's
Steele Glass, a Satyre, 4to. 1576, wherein he has
these words : "The more particular reason (of
sending that poem) is the recommendatory lines
(before it) by Raleigh [2], which may perhaps have
escaped you, though I know your great researches
and acquisitions on his account are beyond whatever has been or is likely to be made again,
wherein you have obliged the learned and curious
world ; and, as you further intend it, I should be
glad to hear that nothing is denied to your ingenious enquiries."

17. Wrote the Dedication of Mr. Hayward's
British Muse to the Lady Mary Wortley Montagu,
which she approved of.

---

[2] As to the internal evidence of this poem being Raleigh's, the critics are at variance. Oldys and Brydges
assume that it is completely in Raleigh's favour: Mr.
D'Israeli, also, though he hesitates about the spelling of
the name [Rawely], says that "these verses, both by
their spirit and signature, cannot fail to be his;" while
Mr. Tytler says, that "although written in the quaint
style of his age, their poetical merit is below his other
pieces, and it is difficult to believe that they flowed from
the same sweet vein which produced the answer to Marlow's Passionate Shepherd." Oldys (*Life of Ralegh*, i.
22., ed. 1829), however, says that "the poem itself, to
me, discovers, in the very first line of it, a great air of
that solid axiomatical vein which is observable in other
productions of Ralegh's muse : —

' Sweet were the sauce would please each kind of taste.' "

18. To remember it be enquired of Mr. Martin[3], what memorials he has, among Mr. Le Neve's papers relating to Norfolk, of Sir John Fastolfe, for augmenting my life of him, which is inserted in the *General Dictionary* [10 vols. fol. 1734–1741.][4] Also to ask Mr. Anstis if he has any further account than what he has publish'd of him. Mr. Locker[5] promised me to borrow of Dr. Rawlinson Father Parsons' (or Cresswell's) Answer to Queen Elizabeth's Proclamation against the Seminary priests, which is a MS., and, as he says, in English, though I never saw any but the Latin one, printed in two or three places abroad, A° 1592, 1593, &c., as I have quoted it in the *Life of Ralegh.* Father Parsons does not deny it to be his, and Watson, in his *Quodlibets* [4to. 1602, p. 107.], often calls it his ; but Lord Coke and other contemporary writers constantly ascribe it to Father Cresswell.[6]

20. To speak with Mr. Birch about an abstract of the Life of Ralegh for the *General Dictionary.* Also to ask him whether, in his late edition of Milton's Prose Works, he has inserted or mentioned *A Copy of a Letter from an Officer of the Armey*

---

[3] Honest Tom Martin of Palgrave: ob. Mar. 7, 1771.

[4] Oldys's Life of Sir John Fastolff was reprinted, with many additions, in the *Biographia Britannica*, 1747—66 ; also in Kippis's, revised by Mr. Gough.

[5] John Locker, Esq. barrister, and commissioner of bankrupts. He is styled by Dr. Johnson "a gentleman eminent for curiosity and literature." Ob. May 29, 1760.

[6] In Dodd's *Church History*, ed. 1739, vol. ii. pp. 405. 419., it is attributed to Robert Parsons as well as to Joseph Creswell. The Bodleian Catalogue has the following note: "Auctor fuit vel Jos. Creswellus vel Rob. Parsons, Jesuita, vel utrique junctim." It is written to prove the lawfulness of rising against what the writer calls an heretic prince, and entitled, " Elizabethæ Angliæ reginæ in Catholicos sui regni edictum, cum responsione ad singula capita ; per D. Andream Philopatrum, presbyte-

in Ireland to his Highness the Lord Protector, con-
cerning the changing of the Government, dated from
Waterford, 24 of June, 1654, in 4to., attested under
the hand of Henry Earl of Clarendon, to be written
by Milton [7] In the Literary Note Book, written
with that Earl's own hand, whence I draw this information, and which is in my possession, there
is also a book entered with this title, which should
be enquired after, *The Life of Edward Lord Her-*
bert, Boron of Cherbury and Castle Islands in Ire-
land, and Knight of the Order of the Bath, written
by himself for the instruction of his posterity
This MS. was lent me (says my Lord) by the
Lady Dowager Herbert, daughter to the Earl of
Bradford, June 11th, 1696.[8]

22. Saw Mr. Ames in the afternoon, and gave
him more materials for Mr. Ward of Sir Thomas
Gresham, from Sir Robert Cotton and David Pa-

---

rum," 8vo. 1592 ; 8vo. et 4to. 1593. A reply to this work was
written in English, entitled " An Advertisement written
to a Secretarie of my L. Treasurer's of Ingland, by an
Inglishe Intelligencer as he passed throughe Germanie
towardes Italie. Anno Dom. 1592." 8vo. Consult also
Miscellanies Historical and Philological, &c. found in a
Nobleman's Study, p. 171, 1703, and Oldys's *Life of Sir
Walter Ralegh,* i. 168., ed. 1829.

[7] This Letter is in the British Museum among the
King's Pamphlets (Press mark 104 a. 10.) It is signed
R. G., and dated " Waterford, 24 June, 1654 ; " but on the
copy in Thomason's collection, he has written " A feigned
date," and has substituted that of 1656 with his pen.
The pamphlet makes 23 pages of 4to. The style is Mil-
tonic. On a copy in the library of Mr. Frederick Hen-
driks, the word *Wellworth* is written in a contemporary
hand. See " N. & Q.," 2ᵈ S. xi. 205.

[8] This book, which Walpole pronounced " the most extraordinary account that was ever given seriously by a
wise man of himself," was first printed at Strawberry
Hill in 1764. For a most amusing account of the manner
in which Walpole obtained the use of the MS., see his
Letter to Montagu of 16th July, 1764. The most complete edition is said to be that published by Jeffrey, London, 1826.

D

pillon.[9]   Bought for him at Bacon's auction,
Arnold's *Chronicle* for 9*s.* 6*d.*, and for Mr. Thomp-
son, John Collins his *Discourse on Salt and
Fishery* [4to. 1682], with the *Treatise of Water-
machines*, for 4*s.* 9*d.*   To dine with him on
Sunday, and meet Dr. Oxley about Cecil's
Letters.

24. Met Mr. Calverley, Hayward, &c., at the
Greyhound Tavern, in the Strand, and they finished
about the Sportsman.   Mr. Hayward to go to .
Andover on Monday the 27th.

26. Dined with Mr. Ames.   Had some talk with
Dr. Oxley and Mr. White about the intended
publication of Cecil's *Letters* [10], and was asked if I
would assist in it.   Understand that they would
publish from the beginning of old Cecil's adminis-
tration to the end of Robert Earl of Salisbury's
Life, 1612; but find that they are inclined to
leave out the letters and testimonies of Princess
Elizabeth's girlish frolicks with Ambrose Dudley.[1]
Were these letters to be fairly published by an
indifferent and unbiassed person who had intimacy
enough with the period of time they comprehend,
to know what would be most needful to complete
the history of it, he might probably find enough
to satisfy the most curious out of this collection.

---

[9] Of David Papillon, Esq., of Acryse or Aukridge, in
Kent, who, after sitting in Parliament for Romney and
Dover, was appointed one of the Commissioners of Excise
in 1742, there is a brief memoir in Nichols's *Literary
Anecdotes*, v. 470., *et seq.*

[10] *A Collection of State Papers left by William Cecil,
Lord Burghley*, edited by Samuel Haynes, A.M. fol. 1740.

[1] Afterwards Baron L'Isle and Earl of Warwick.   Probably Oldys was thinking of Elizabeth's girlish tricks
with Sir Thomas Seymour (Lord Seymour of Sudley)
which are not suppressed in the *Burghley State Papers*
(see pp. 99—102.).   Lord Seymour made his addresses to
the Princess Elizabeth with so much warmth that the
Council found it necessary to interfere, and the deposi-
tions of several persons taken on that occasion have been
preserved by Haynes in the above work.

But where many important things must be stifled
in favour to the character of one man, History
descends as corrupted to posterity through the
wilful partiality of the knowing, as through all
the involuntary imperfections of ignorance.

31. Much talk with Mr. Jernegan[2] about his
late lottery; the troubles and opposition he has
had in it; by what means he avoided the Act of
Parliament; how the ladies stood his friend; and
upon what proffer his fine bason and ewer, which
was at first so much admired by Lord B—n, came
to be slighted. Also why he made those emblems
upon his medals, rather than a representation of
the great cistern or himself upon them. Also of
the talents of Vanloo[3], the portrait painter, so
much in vogue now at court; and concerning a
print to be made of Capt. Robert Jenkins, who
had his ear cut off by the Spaniards[4]; and, lastly,
of his strange projects to prevent all disputes in
religion, provide fortunes for all younger sons,

---

[2] Mr. Henry Jernegan, fourth son of Sir Francis Jer-
ningham or Jernegan. of Cossey, in Norfolk, a goldsmith
and jeweller, in Russell Street, made a curious silver cistern (of which there is a fine engraving by Vertue), which
was disposed of by lottery about the year 1740. The
price of a ticket was five or six shillings, and the pur-
chaser had a silver medal worth about three shillings
into the bargain. There were 30,000 tickets, and the
medals induced many people to buy them. He died 8th
Nov. 1761, and was buried at St. Paul's, Covent Garden.
See Nichols's *Lit. Anec.* ii. 513.

[3] This was John Baptist Vanloo, who came to London
in 1737, and whose portraits of Colley Cibber and Mac
Swinney the actor, procured him the patronage of the
Prince and Princess of Wales and Sir Robert Walpole.

[4] In June, 1731, the *Rebecca*, commanded by Capt.
Jenkins, was taken in her passage from Jamaica by a
Spanish Guarde Costa, who put all on board to the tor-
ture. The captain was hung up three times, once with a
cabin boy at his feet, and afterwards had one of his ears
cut off, bidding him to carry it to his king, and tell his
majesty, that if he were present they would use him in
the same manner. — *Gent. Mag.* i. 265.; viii. 336.

and marry all the daughters without any portions.
He certainly is a pleasant man in his nature, of an
open, generous, and brave spirit, and no wonder
he should be somewhat conceited, or strive by
uncommon flights and fancies to make the abilities of his mind appear extraordinary, who has
been by nature so liberally endowed with those of
the body, having been a man of the greatest
agility in his time, very personable; and it is
much his elegant form and features are not more
declined, considering how much he has been lately
harassed by this troublesome engagement; how
much more possibly by his amours and gallantries;
and that though he yet appears not above forty,
he is drawing on towards fifty years of age.

Apr. 6. Passed some time with Mr. Caban very
merrily; promis'd to come and bring the French
Books he so much recommends. To enquire more
particularly about the translator of Milton's *Paradise Lost* into French, with whom he seems to
have been acquainted when he was last in France.

14. Mr. Vertue called. Memorandum, when I
write to Mr. Hayward, to mention the plays Lady
Mary Wortley Montagu was to have had of him
for Lady Pomfret.

20. Remember to go with Mr. Ames to Mr.
Pate[5] to get a sight of some observations he has
in manuscript on *The History of the Three Impostors*.[6] Mr. Lewis his *Life of Caxton* to be out
in three weeks.

---

[5] William Pate, the friend of Dean Swift, who lived
over against the Royal Exchange, and was commonly
called "the learned tradesman." In 1734 he was one of
the sheriffs of London, and died in 1746. — Nichols's *Lit.
Anec.* i. 99.

[6] Oldys here alludes to the *Crux Bibliographica*, the
famous tract *De Tribus Impostoribus*, on the existence
and author (styled by Sir Thomas Browne "*that villain
and Secretary of Hell*,") of which so many disputes have
been moved by the bibliographers of the last century.—
Mr. James Crossley, in "N. & Q.," 2nd S. xi. 204.

22. The merry Gascon promised to procure me of Capt. Le Croise a sight of the famous book called *The History of the Three Impostors*, the manuscript whereof is valued at five guineas. The French manuscript is a translation, or pretends to be so, from the Latin; and has a French dissertation upon it prefixed, which, by the beginning, whereof he shewed me a copy, should be the same as that Mr. Ames talks of.

28. Finished the Catalogue of my English Lives, 8vo. in 74 pages, concerning above 200 English persons. Mr. Caban, among the French authors he brought for me, did lend me one somewhat like Mr. Hayward's Collection in three volumes, but is far from being so general or various; for the French collection is confined chiefly to love, as the very title declares, being called *Sentimens d'Amour tirez des Meilleurs Poëtes Modernes, par le Sieur Corbinelli*, 2 vols. 8vo. Paris, 1665.

May 15. Paid Mr. Ames yesterday, being Sunday, at his house, for two copies of Mr. Lewis's *Life of Caxton*, 10s.

Mar. 1. [1739 ?] Bid 35 guineas and a half for a conversation piece which had Tenier's name painted upon it, at Cock's auction of Mons. Beauvais' Collection of Curiosities, for his Lordship [Oxford]. But Sir Paul Methuen got it for 36 guineas. Gave his Lordship my manuscript of Sir Fra. Walsingham's Table Book.

4. Left my poem on the Peace with Mr. C. [Coxeter ?]

15. Met the Committee, &c., at the Crown and Anchor Tavern, against St. Clement's church: Mr. Broughton and Mr. Campbell there.

21. Dined with my Lord according to his invitation by letter yesterday; Lord Duplin there, and Duke of Portland.

27. Received 20l. of Lord Oxford to lay out; and promise of 200l. per annum as secretary.

CHOICE NOTES.

BY WILLIAM OLDYS.

As supplementary to the curious fragment of a Diary by William Oldys, we have now the pleasure of presenting to our readers a few Choice Notes from his manuscript Adversaria, which may not be without their value and instruction to the student of Biography and Bibliography. Every man of letters, but especially the lovers of our early English literature, may learn something from the literary researches of this indefatigable antiquary. By the publication of his valuable work, *The British Librarian*, Oldys was among the first to direct public attention to the old and valuable literature of our country, by collecting materials for its literary history during the Middle Ages. So true is the quaint and beautiful teaching of Chaucer —

> " For out of the olde fieldes, as men saithe,
> Cometh all this newe corn fro yere to yere,
> And out of olde bookes, in good faithe,
> Cometh all this newe science that men lere."

Ardently devoted from his early days to the pursuit of literature, and secluded in some degree from the world, we can only get a glimpse of Oldys's personal history and habits of life from those curious memoranda which have escaped destruction, and which may occasionally be discovered in public and private libraries.—ED.

" July 20, 1749.—Was informed this day by M[r]. Thomas Odell's daughter that her father, who was Deputy Licenser of the Plays, died the 24th May, 1749, at his house in Chapel Street, Westminster, of the gout in his stomach, aged 58 years, and was buried in Chapel Churchyard, Westmin-

ster. He was writing An History of the Characters he had observed, and Conferences he had held
with many eminent persons he had known in his
time. He was a great observator of everything
curious in the conversation of his acquaintance ;
and his own conversation was a living chronicle
of the remarkable intrigues, adventures, sayings,
stories, writings, &c. of many of the Quality,
Poets, and other Authors, Players, Booksellers,
&c. who flourished especially in the present century. He had been a popular man at elections,
and sometime Master of the Playhouse in Goodman's Fields ; but latterly was forced to live reserved and retired by reason of his debts. He
published two or three dramatic pieces." [1]

July 31. Was at Mrs. Odell's in Chapel Street,
Westminster. She returned me Mr. Budgell's
papers. Saw several of her late husband's papers,
mostly Poems in favour of the Ministry, and
against Mr. Pope. One of them printed by the
late Sir Robert Walpole's encouragement, who
gave him ten guineas for writing, and as much for
the expense of printing it; but through his advice
it was never published, because it might hurt
his interest with Lord Chesterfield and some other
noblemen who favoured Mr. Pope for his fine
genius. The tract I liked best of his writings,
was the History of his Play-house in Goodman's
Fields. [Remember that which was published
against that playhouse, which I have entered in
my London Catalogue [2]]. Saw nothing of the

---

[1] Odell is noticed in Baker's *Biographia Dramatica*,
s. v., where it is stated that " he brought four dramatic
pieces on the stage, all of which met with some share of
success. Their titles are as follows : *Chimera*, Com. 1721.
Patron. Opera, *n. d.* *Smugglers*, Farce, 1729. *Prodigal*,
Com. 1744." The copyright of *The Prodigal* was assigned
to Watts for twelve guineas on 9th October, 1744.

[2] Letter to Sir Richard Brocas, Lord Mayor, 8vo.
1730. [By Dr. Francis Hare, Bishop of Chichester.]

History of his Conversations with Ingenious Men ;
his Characters, Tales, Jests, and Intrigues of
them, of which no man was better furnished with
them. She thinks she has some papers of them,
and promises to look them out, and also to enquire
after Mr. Griffin, of the Lord Chamberlain's office, that I may get a search made about Spenser.

Sept. 27, 1749. Mr. Vertue sent me a transcript
of King Charles his Patent to Ben Jonson for 100*l.*
per annum. Also extracts from the accounts of
Lord Stanhope, Treasurer of the Chamber to
King James, from the Year 1613 to 1616, relating
to the payment of the Players for acting of Plays
in and between those Years at Court. Also Mr.
Robinson sent me part of his Letter in print to
the Speaker, Arthur Onslow.[3] Remember the
story of the 350*l.* in Bank bills found in a volume
of Archbishop Tillotson's Sermons by the executor
of Sir Simon Urlin, whose books and money they
had been. Of Alexander Ross, his treasure in
old gold found between the covers of his library.

DRYDEN.—Remember my large bundle of Pamphlets, all written by, for, or against Mr. Dryden, in
fol., 4to., and 8vo. And my Chronological Draught
or Skeleton of his Personal Story, to be enlarged
into a Life of him, when that shall be published,
which is to be written by Mr. Broughton for the
Biographia Britannica.
To search the old papers in one of my large
deal boxes for Mr. Dryden's letter of thanks to
my father, for some communications relating to
Plutarch, when they and others were publishing

---

[3] " The Case of the Chief Justice of Gibraltar, truly
and impartially stated, in a Letter address'd by him to
the Right Hon. Arthur Onslow, Esq., Speaker of the
House of Commons." 8vo. It is signed Robert Robinson, who was, for a short period, Chief Justice of Gibraltar,
and dated Lincoln's Inn, 30 Nov. 1749.

a translation of all Plutarch's *Lives* in 5 vols.
8vo. 1683.

Mr. Dryden's Poem to King William, of which
I have two copies in MS., with a Discourse prefixed, containing an Apology for his past Life and
Writings, dedicated to the Lord Dorset, appears
not likely to be of his writing, but rather an im-
position on the world in his name, to expose the
inconstancy of his principles.[4]

The story of Mr. Dryden's dream at Lord Exeter's at Burleigh, while he was translating Virgil,
as Signor Verrio, then painting there, related it
to the Yorkshire painter, of whom I had it, lies in
the parchment-book in quarto, designed for his
Life. . . . Now entered therein.

See my life of Mary, Countess of Pembroke, in
the Parchment budget of Biography. I lent her
play [*Antonius*], &c., to Mr. Collins to help him
in her Life: then gave the book to Mr. Coxeter.

Old Counsellor Fane of Colchester, who, *in
formâ pauperis*, deceived me of a good sum of
money which he owed me, and not long after set
up his chariot, gave me a parcel of manuscripts,
and promised me among others (which he never
gave me, nor anything else, besides a barrel of
oysters), a manuscript copy of Randolph's *Poems*
—an original, as he said, with many additions,
never printed, being devolved to him as the
author's relation.

See my account of the Life of Thomas Rawlins
in the little paper book, 12mo., among the poets
in the Biographical Budget. — Remember in my
first volume of Poetical Characteristics the epitaph on Mr. Rawlins.[5]

---

[4] See Malone's Life of John Dryden, *Prose Works*, i.
422., ed. 1800.

[5] Thomas Rawlins was engraver to the Mint, and died
in that employment in 1670. He was author of a tragedy

It has been affirmed to me, that Samuel Cooper, the miniature painter, would steal a face upon his nail; and remember the complexion, air, and all other distinguishments, so exactly, as to present any person with their portrait, who never knew they had sat to him for it.

I gave above threescore letters of Dr. Davenant to his son, who was envoy at Frankfort in 1703 to 1708, to Mr. James West[6], with one hundred and fifty more, about Christmas, 1746; but the same fate they found as grain that is sowed in barren ground.

I lent the tragical lives and deaths of the famous pirates, Ward & Dansiker, 4to., London, 1612, by Robert Daborn *alias* Dabourne, to Mr. T. Lediard, when he was writing his *Naval History*, and he never returned it. See Howel's *Letters* of them.

The famous Queen Elizabeth's old mulberry tree, with a large head and spacious arms upheld by props, like the pages that supported her train, now growing with other large trees of that kind in one of the gardens at Carlisle House in Lambeth Marsh, and full of fruit this July, 1753. It has the most reverend marks of antiquity upon it of any tree I ever saw of the kind. It had been split by the weight of its own shade and fruit, but is braced at the upper part of the trunk with iron. The shade may be near forty yards in circumference. The fruit is rich. Four hundred pottles were gathered when I saw it about Sep-

called *Rebellion*, 1640, 4to., and again 1654, 4to. He also published (says Oldys) a book of Poems, under the title of *Culanthe*, 8vo., 1648; and likewise, if not the same, *Good Friday; or, Divine Meditations on the Passion of Christ*, and with it some other small pieces of poetry, 4to., 1663.

    [6] See *antè*, p. 3.

tember that year, and probably another hundred
left. The ground, all under and about the tree,
looked as if all bloody by people treading upon
the fallen fruit.

See my account of the great yews in Tankersly
Park, Yorkshire, while Sir Richard Fanshaw was
prisoner in the Lodge there in 1655, in my bota-
nical budget : especially Talbot's Yew, which a
man on horseback might turn about in.

Old Lady Viscountess de Longueville (grand-
mother to the Earl of Sussex, who died in 1763,
aged near 100,) has told me, that she well remembered Mr. Dryden's dining with her husband at
their house in town. The most remarkable thing
she recollected of his figure was an uncommon
distance between his eyes. This old lady was a
living chronicle, and retained the most perfect
memory to the very last : was daughter of Sir
John Talbot of Lacocke ; had been Maid of
Honour to Queen Anne, when Princess of Denmark (she had a daughter, afterwards Maid of
Honour to her when Queen,) before the Revolu-
tion, at which time she went with the Court (the
Queen, if I remember right,) to pay a visit to
Mr. Waller, the poet, at his seat at Becconsfield ;
at which time, although he was very old, he received them with great gallantry and politeness.
Mr. Waller was then above eighty, Lady Longueville survived him seventy-six years. Here we
have an instance of two persons only that could
have carried down the memory of any fact more
than 150 years without any intermediate reporters.
A remarkable instance ! [7]

[7] We happen to know of another remarkable instance.
James Stuart, the architect (better known as the Athe-
nian Stuart), died on the 1st February, 1788, aged 76.
His son, Commander James Stuart, R.N., was born on
the 13th April following, and is still living, honoured and

Lady Longueville's father had a house in Pall
Mall, not far from the Duchess of Mazarine's.
She well remembered Mons. Sieg. Evremont, a
little old man in his black silk coif, who was used
to be carried every morning by their window in a
sedan-chair to the Dutchess's house, at which time
he always took with him a pound of butter made
in his own little dairy, for her Grace's breakfast.

This old lady remembered the time when the
fashionable hour of dining was twelve o'clock,
and when the plays begun at three in the afternoon. The interest of her fortune had brought
her in ten per cent. She was used to tell many
bon-mots of Charles II. Her father was one day
going down to Whitehall with his lady, and met
the King in the Mall in St. James's Park. " So,
Jack," says the King, "where are you going?"
" To Whitehall Chapel to prayers," said he.
" Well," said the other, "and have you taken
care to carry your wife's Prayer-book in your
pocket?"

This old lady had an hereditary attachment to
the House of Stuart; yet she frankly acknow-
ledged that Bishop Burnet's *History of his Own
Time* gave a very exact and true account of the
state of the Court, agreeably to her own notions
and remembrance.

The said Charles II.'s dying request to his brother was " to take care of Carewell " (meaning
Madame Querouaille, Duchess of Portsmouth, pronounced *Carewell* by the English,) "and not let
poor Nelly (meaning Nell Gwin) starve."[8]

---

respected by all his friends, in the vicinity of Epping-
forest. The architect, born in the reign of Queen Anne,
may have seen the great Duke of Marlborough, as his
son assuredly has, on many occasions, both seen and admired the late Arthur, Duke of Wellington.

[8] Thus far Oldys. Bishop Percy has added the following additional note: —

" She was wont to tell many little anecdotes of Charles

SIR EDWARD DYER, a man of fine parts and ac-
complishments, was a dependant upon the Court
in Queen Elizabeth's reign, but one of those who
would not fawn and cringe, and long had expec-
tations given him from her of preferment suitable
to his merits. It happened as he was one day
walking under her window that Her Majesty was
looking out, and seeing him in a very pensive
mood, she had a mind to be jocose. "Sir Edward, Sir Edward," says she, "what does a man
think of when he thinks of Nothing?" "A woman's promise," answered he with a smile. The
Queen shrunk in her head, and said to somebody
near her, "Well, this anger would be a brave passion for making men witty, if it was not so base a
one as keep them poor." [9]

II.'s Queen, whom she described as a little ungraceful
woman: so short-legged, that when she stood upon her
feet you would have thought she was on her knees; and
yet so long-waisted, that when she sat down, she appeared a well-sized woman. Her mother's father was
Sir Henry Slingsby, who was beheaded in the Great Rebellion. She was related to the Duchess of Buckingham,
Lord Fairfax's daughter, whom she described to be much
such another in person as the Queen Catherine, a little
round crumpled woman, very fond of finery. She remembered paying her a visit, when she (the Duchess) was in
mourning, at which time she found her lying on a sopha,
with a kind of loose robe over her, all edged or laced
with gold. This I mention because Fairfax, in his Life
of the Duke of Buckingham, says 'if she had some of the
vanities, she had none of the vices of her sex.' "
9 Sir Edward Dyer had most probably recently published his tract *The Prayse of Nothing*. By E. D. Imprinted at London, in Fleete-streate, beneath the Con-
duite, at the signe of S. John Euangelist, by H. Jackson,
1585, of which the only copy known is preserved in the
Bodleian library, among the books of Bishop Tanner.
This tract has been privately reprinted by Mr. J. P.
Collier, the impression limited to 25 copies, which cost,
including the binding, 12l. 10s., that is 10s. per copy. Pp.
44. 4to.

E

WANLEY.— All the account of the Harleian library [in Nicolson's *Historical Libraries*, 1736,
p. vi.], was written by Mr. Humphry Wanley,
librarian to the Lord Treasurer Harley, as his
son, the most noble Edward, Earl of Oxford, my
most invaluable friend and patron, informed me
in the year 1730; but it would make a volume
as big as this to give a just idea of this library.
Mr. Wanley died July 6, 1726.   See the Diary of
his own Life in the Harleian library.

QUEEN ANNE.—When the Lord Treasurer Oxford recommended Sir Symonds D'Ewes' manuscripts to be purchased by Queen Anne for a
public library, as the richest collection in England
next to Sir Robert Cotton's, she said, " It was no
virtue for her, a woman, to prefer as she did, arts
to arms; but while the blood and honour of the
nation was at stake in her wars, she could not,
till she had secured her *living* subjects an honourable peace, bestow their money upon *dead* letters." Whereupon the Earl stretched his own
purse, and gave 6000*l*. for the library.

" TRINARCHODIA."— In a manuscript volume,
formerly in the possession of James Petit Andrews, Esq., entitled *Trinarchodia: the severall
Raignes of Richard the Second, Henrie the Fourth,
and Henrie the Fifth*, is the following note by
Wm. Oldys, who appears to have been its former
possessor : — " By what I can find, in perusing
this book, so full of uncouth and obscure phrases,
metaphorical allusions, distant, abstracted conceits, and mystical learning, the author was a
clergyman, and calls King Charles II. his master.
He began this book on the 7th Nov. 1649, and
ended it on All Souls' Day, 1650.   It further
seems, these three reigns and the *Idyllia* were
written for the press ; but not to be published
till after his death, and then without his name ;

yet the *Idyllia*, by being said to be revised and enlarged, looks as if it had been published before."

BROWNE. — William Browne [author of *Britannia's Pastorals*] was reputed a man not only the best versed in the works and beauties of the English poets, but also in the history of their lives and characters : wherefore he was pitched upon to draw out the line of his poetic ancestors, from Josephus Iscanius down to himself, which must have been a delectable and useful labour, from a man not only of his learning and taste, but who had the advantage of living so much nearer the times when our most renowned cultivators of English poetry adorned this isle.[10]

CHAUCER'S PORTRAIT. — Winstanley, in his *Lives of the Poets*, p. 26., says, " Thomas Occleve, of the office of the privy seal, sometime Chaucer's scholar, for the love he bore him, caused his picture to be truly drawn in his book *De regimine principis ;* according to which, that his picture drawn upon his monument was made." To this passage Mr. Oldys added the following note in the margin of his copy of Winstanley — " This book, *De regimine principis,* a pretty thick folio, written, in English stanzas, on vellum, with that picture of Chaucer on the side of the verses, is in the possession of Mr. West of the Temple, who showed it me, Feb. 27, 1735."[1]

---

10 An edition of Wm. Browne's Works was published by Thomas Davies in 1772, 3 vols. 12mo., with some short notes by the Rev. William Thompson.

1 Some curious particulars of this portrait of Chaucer are given in Kippis's *Biog. Britan.* iii. 465. 467.; Walpole's *Anecdotes of Painting,* ed. 1849, i. 30.; *Gent. Mag.* Oct. 1841, p. 370.; and in Warton's *History of English Poetry,* ii. 263. Mr. Warton informs us, that " it is in one of the Royal manuscripts of Occleve's poem in the British Museum that he has left a drawing of Chaucer; according to which, Chaucer's portraiture was made on his

CHURCHYARD.—Thomas Churchyard, who was
called the old Court Poet almost all Queen Elizabeth's reign, was a gentleman born: by his studies at
Oxford and his travels, a man of learning and experience : by his services and sufferings in the wars, a
man of valour and merit: by his attendance on courts
and great men, a man of manners, address, polite
conversation, and other engaging qualities; and
with all this he died a beggar, without ever having it in his power to make himself so by extra-
vagance. All who have spoken of him know
little of his story, as Fuller, Winstanley, and even
Anthony Wood, who says, he laboured much to
recover the titles of his writings, in that very imperfect catalogue he gives us of them in his life.
[Wood's *Athenæ*, by Bliss, i. 727.] But from some
of them he never saw we collect, he was born in
Shrewsbury about the year 1520; came to Henry's
court in 1537 ; had served in the wars abroad ;
and was subject at home under eight [?] crowned
heads : had also been in the service of two or
three of the noblest families in England : had dedicated books and pamphlets, in poetry and prose,
of his own composing and translation, from Latin
and some modern languages, to above twenty
great personages of fortune and distinction : most
generously recorded the praises and celebrated
the memories of half the great men of his time.
Yet with all his fighting and writing ; loss of

monument, in the chapel of St. Blase in Westminster
Abbey, by the benefaction of Nicholas Brigham, in the
year 1556. From this drawing, in 1598, John Speed procured the print of Chaucer prefixed to Speght's edition of
his *Works* ; which has since been copied in a most finished
engraving by Vertue in Urry's edition, 1721, fol. Yet it
must be remembered that the same drawing occurs in the
Harleian MS. 4866. fol. 91., written about Occleve's age,
and in the Cotton. MS. Oth. A. 18. Occleve himself mentions this drawing in his *Consolatio Servilis*. It exactly
resembles the curious picture on board of our venerable
bard, preserved in the Bodleian gallery at Oxford."

much blood and time in camps and courts, in a
fearful and fruitless attendance and dependence
upon the ungrateful great for above sixty-seven
years, never could get more than a scanty pension
from Queen Elizabeth[2], and that, according to
his own words, seems to have been through the
interest of Sir Walter Ralegh ; but so scanty,
that upon the death of Dr. John Underhill, Bishop
of Oxford, one of his best friends, he had no better prospect or resource, in 1592, of sustaining
himself to the end of his natural course, than ex-
posing again his aged and scarified limbs to the
hardships of war in foreign service, as he miser-
ably complains in his poem of *The Unhappy Man'
Dear Adieu.* He did struggle on, abroad and at
home, to salute King James with a congratulation
soon after his entrance and coronation[3], anno 1604
[1603 ?], when he could not be less than eighty-four
years of age, if not more. What notice was then
taken of him we find not, nor when he died, but
it could not be long after[4], when somebody did
cover his bones in Westminster Abbey, and hide
as much as they could such a shameful monument
and testimony to their country of the ingratitude
that reigns in courts and courtiers, in masters and
patrons, towards their servants and dependants.

---

[2] See " *A Pleasant Conceite*, penned in verse, collour-
ably sette ont, and humblie presented, on New-yeere's
day last, to the Queene's Majestie at Hampton Court,
anno Domini 1593–4," printed in Nichols's *Progresses of
Queen Elizabeth*, iii. 232.

[3] *A Pæan Triumphal upon the King's Entry to London
from the Tower.* 1603.

[4] Arrived at length at the advanced age of eighty-
four, Churchyard died in Westminster about the 1st of
April, 1604, and was certainly buried, as the parish
register evinces, on the 4th day of the same month, in
the quire of St. Margaret's Church, near his favourite
Skelton, and not in the church-porch, according to a
ludicrous epitaph in Camden's *Remains.* — George Chalmers's Life of him in *Churchyard's Chips*, 8vo. 1817.

E 3

SHADWELL. — The character of Capt. Hackum,
in Thomas Shadwell's comedy *The Squire of Al-
satia*, was drawn (as I have been told by old John
Bowman the player) to expose Bully Dawson, a
noted sharper, swaggerer, and debauchee, about
town, especially Blackfriars and its infamous pur-
lieus.

Tom Shadwell died suddenly of an apoplexy
(or by taking too large a dose of opium given him
by mistake) at Chelsea, near London, Nov. 20,
1692, in the fifty-third year of his age, and was
buried in the church there the 25th of the same
month. See his Funeral Sermon by Nich. Brady,
4to. 1693.

If Shadwell could not match Ben Jonson in his
learning, in the deep reach of his plots, the inno-
cence of his humorous characters, and the chastity
of his morals, and other qualifications of his mind,
he did at least in the corpulency of his body.
Whence among many other sarcasms, we may account for this extraordinary epitaph of Tom
Brown : —

> " And must our glorious Laureat then depart?
> Heav'n, if it please, may take his loyal heart;
> As for the rest, sweet Devil, bring a cart."

SPENSER. — Ask Sir Peter Thompson if it were
improper to try if Lord Effingham Howard would
procure the pedigrees in the Heralds' office, to be
seen for Edward Spenser's parentage or family;
or how he was related to Sir John Spenser of
Althorpe, in Northamptonshire, to three of whose
daughters, who all married nobility, Spenser de-
dicates three of his poems.

Of Mr. Vertue, to examine Stow's memorandum book. Look more carefully for the year
when Spenser's monument was raised, or between
which years the entry stands — 1623 and 1626.

Sir Clement Cottrell's book about Spenser.

Capt. Power, to know if he has heard from

Capt. Spenser about my letter of inquiries relating to Edward Spenser.

Of Whiston, to examine if my remarks on Spenser are complete as to the press. — Yes.

Remember when I see Mr. William Thompson [5], to inquire whether he has printed in any of his works any other character of our old poets than those of Spenser and Shakspeare ; and to get the liberty of a visit at Kentish Town, to see his collections of Robert Greene's works, in about four large volumes of quarto. He commonly published a pamphlet every term, as his acquaintance Tom Nash informs us.

SHAKSPEARE. — There was a very aged gentleman living in the neighbourhood of Stratford (where he died fifty years since) who had not only heard, from several old people in the town, of Shakspeare's transgression, but could remember the first stanza of that bitter ballad, which, repeating to one of his acquaintance, he preserved it in writing ; and here it is neither better nor worse, but faithfully transcribed from the copy

---

[5] William Thompson, a warm lover of our elder bards, and no vulgar imitator of Spenser, was the second son of the Rev. Francis Thompson, Rector of Brough in Westmoreland. He was entered as a scholar at Queen's College, Oxford, where he graduated A.M. in 1738. He afterwards became fellow of the same college, and succeeded to the livings of Weston and Hampton Poyle in Oxfordshire; after which (according to Alex. Chalmers) he became Dean of Raphoe in Ireland, where he died about 1766. D'Israeli informs us, that "he was the reviver of Bishop Hall's *Satires* in 1753, by an edition which had been more fortunate if conducted by his friend Oldys, for the text is unfaithful, though the edition followed was one borrowed from Lord Oxford's library, probably by the aid of Oldys." In 1757, Thompson published two volumes of *Poems*, among which those entitled " The Nativity ; " " Sickness ; " and " The Hymn to May," have met with considerable approbation.

which his relation very courteously communicated
to me [6] : —

> " A parliemente member, a justice of peace,
> At home a poor scare-crowe, at London an asse;
> If lowsie is Lucy, as some volke miscalle it,
> Then Lucy is lowsie whatever befall it:
>   He thinks himself greate,
>   Yet an' asse in his state,
> We allowe by his ears but with asses to mate.
> If Lucy is lowsie, as some volke miscalle it,
> Sing lowsie Lucy, whatever befall it."

If tradition may be trusted, Shakspeare often
baited at the Crown Inn or tavern in Oxford, in
his journey to and from London.[7] The landlady
was a woman of great beauty and sprightly wit,
and her husband, Mr. John Davenant (afterwards
mayor of that city), a grave melancholy man,
who, as well as his wife, used much to delight in
Shakspeare's pleasant company. Their son, young
Will. Davenant (afterwards Sir William) was then
a little school-boy in the town [8], of about seven or
eight years old, and so fond also of Shakspeare,
that whenever he heard of his arrival, he would
fly from school to see him. One day an old townsman observing the boy running homeward almost

---

[6] According to Mr. Capell, this ballad came originally
from Mr. Thomas Jones, who lived at Tarbick, a village
about eighteen miles from Stratford-upon-Avon, and died
in 1703, aged upwards of ninety. Mr. Wilkes (adds Malone) grandson of the gentleman to whom Mr. Jones repeated this first stanza of the ballad, appears to have been
the person who gave a copy of it to Mr. Oldys and Mr.
Capell. " What is called a ' complete copy of the verses '
contained in Malone's Shakspeare by Boswell, vol. ii. p.
565., is evidently not genuine." (Collier's *Shakspeare*,
ed. 1858, i. 70.) See also Halliwell's *Shakspeare*, p. 129,
130. ; and Malone's *Shakspeare*, by Boswell, ii. 140.

[7] See Wood's *Athenæ*, iii. 802. (Blias) for the anecdote
of Shakspeare stopping at the Crown Inn, at Oxford.

[8] He was born at Oxford in February, 1605-6, and on
the 3rd of March following, was baptized at St. Martin's Church, in which parish his father's house stood.

out of breath, asked him whither he was posting
in that heat and hurry.   He answered, To see his
god-father Shakspeare.   "There is good boy," said
the other, "but have a care that you don't take   ·
God's name in vain."   This story Mr. Pope told
me at the Earl of Oxford's table, upon occasion
of some discourse which arose about Shakspeare's
monument, then newly erected in Westminster
Abbey ; and he quoted Mr. Betterton the player
for his authority.   I answered, that I thought
such a story might have enriched the variety of
those choice fruits of observation he has presented
us in his Preface to the edition he had published
of our Poet's works.   He replied, " There might
be in the garden of mankind such plants as would
seem to pride themselves more in a regular production of their own native fruits, than in having
the repute of bearing a richer kind by grafting ;
and this was the reason he omitted it."[9]

One of Shakspeare's younger brothers, who
lived to a good old age, even some years as I
compute, after the restoration of King Charles II.,
would in his younger days come to London to
visit his brother *Will*, as he called him, and be a

---

[9] Mr. Oldys might have added, that *he* was the person
who suggested to Mr. Pope the singular course which he
pursued in his edition of Shakspeare.   "Remember,"
says Oldys, in his annotated Langbaine, art. Shakspeare,
" what I observed to my Lord Oxford for Mr. Pope's use,
out of the Cowley's preface."   See Cowley's *Works*, Preface, p. 53. ed. 1710, 8vo., where he says, " This has been
the case with Shakspeare, Fletcher, Jonson, and others,
part of whose poems I should presume to take the bold-
ness *to prune and lop away*, if the care of replanting them
in print did belong to me."   Pope adopted this unwar-
rantable idea; striking out from the text of his author
whatever he did not like; and Cowley himself has suffered a sort of poetical punishment for having suggested
it, the learned Bishop Hurd having pruned and lopped
away his beautiful luxuriances, as Pope, on Cowley's
suggestion, did those of Shakspeare. — *Malone.*

spectator of him as an actor in some of his own plays. This custom, as his brother's fame enlarged, and his dramatick entertainments grew the greatest support of our principal, if not of all our theatres, he continued, it seems, so long after his brother's death, as even to the latter end of his own life. The curiosity at this time of the most noted actors [exciting them] to learn something from him of his brother, &c., they justly held him in the highest veneration. And it may be well believed, as there was besides a kinsman and descendant of the family, who was then a celebrated actor among them[10], this opportunity made them greedily inquisitive into every little circumstance, more especially in his dramatick character, which his brother could relate of him. But he, it seems, was so stricken in years, and possibly his memory so weakened with infirmities (which might make him the easier pass for a man of weak intellects), that he could give them but little light into their inquiries; and all that could be recollected from him of his brother *Will* in that station was, the faint, general, and almost lost ideas he had of having once seen him act a part in one of his own comedies, wherein being to personate a decrepit old man, he wore a long beard, and appeared so weak and drooping and unable to walk, that he was forced to be supported and carried by another person to a table, at which he was seated among some company, who were eating, and one of them sung a song.[1]

Verses by Ben Jonson and Shakspeare, occa-

---

[10] Charles Hart, the actor, was born about the year 1630, and died in August, 1683. If he was a grandson of Shakespeare's sister, he was probably the son of Michael Hart, her youngest son. — *Malone.*

[1] See the character of Adam in *As You like it*, Act II. Sc. *ult.*

sioned by the motto to the Globe Theatre— *Totus mundus agit histrionem :* —

Jonson.

" If, but *stage actors,* all the world displays,
Where shall we find *spectators* of their plays? "

Shakspeare.

" Little, or much, of what we see, we do;
We are all both *actors* and *spectators* too."

Poetical Characteristicks, 8vo. MS. vol. i., some-time in the Harleian library ; which volume was returned to its owner.

Old Mr. Bowman, the player, reported from Sir William Bishop, that some part of Sir John Falstaff's character was drawn from a townsman of Stratford, who either faithlessly broke a con-tract, or spitefully refused to part with some land for a valuable consideration, adjoining to Shak-speare's, in or near that town.

King James the First honoured Shakspeare with an epistolary correspondence ; and I think Sir William D'Avenant had either seen or was possessed of his Majesty's letter to him. See Pre-face to Lintot's edition of his *Poems.*[2]

A probable computation of the thousands of people of both sexes whom Shakspeare's Plays

---

[2] At the conclusion of the advertisement prefixed to Lintot's edition of Shakspeare's *Poems,* it is said, " That most learned prince, and great patron of learning, King James the First, was pleased with his own hand to write an amicable letter to Mr. Shakspeare; which letter, though now lost, remained long in the hands of Sir Wil-liam D'Avenant, as a credible person now living can testify." Mr. Oldys, in a manuscript note to his copy of Fuller's *Worthies,* observes, that "the story came from the Duke of Buckingham, who had it from Sir William D'Avenant." Dr. Farmer, with great probability, sup-poses that this letter was written by King James in re-turn for the compliment paid to him in *Macbeth.* The relater of this anecdote was Sheffield, Duke of Bucking-ham. — *Malone.*

have maintained to this day, would appear in-
credible to anyone who did not maturely consider it.

ATKYNS'S GLOUCESTERSHIRE.—There was copy
enough for two large volumes in folio, though we
have but one. The original manuscript of the
second volume, together with many printed copies
of the first, being all accidentally burnt in the
fire that happened at Mr. Bowyer's house [Jan.
29, 1712-13], in which the first volume was
printed, and the second was at the press.[3]

BEHN. — See my account of her Life in the
parchment volume, 4to., also in the *General Dictionary*; and now by Parson Broughton, in *Biog.
Britannica*, 1746. See several of her Posthumous
Poems in the *Muses' Mercury, or Monthly Miscellany*, 4to. 1707, which have not been taken notice of in any account of her.

Mrs. Behn translated one of the books of Cowley's Latin poem on Plants. In this translation,
when she comes to Daphne, who was turned into
the Bay-tree, she makes the following insertion of
her own : —

> " I, by a double right, thy bounties claim,
> Both from my sex, and in Apollo's name.
> Let me with Sappho and Orinda be,
> Oh ever sacred nymph, adorned by thee, ⎱
> And give my verses immortality."   ⎰

See what Tate in his Preface, and Dryden says
of her, and Capt. Alexander Radcliff in my Life
of her and Prior. About a dozen lines against
her in the Satire on Translators, first printed in

---

[3] The plates of Atkyns's *Gloucestershire*, except two
or three, having escaped the fire of Mr. Bowyer's printing-
office in White Friars, the work was republished in 1768
by Wm. Herbert, the editor of Ames's *Typog. Antiquities*;
but by a singular fatality, a great part of this second
edition was also destroyed by fire. Nichols's *Lit. Anec.*
v. 266.)

the *State Poems* [4to. 1689], then in R. Cross's *Collection of Poems*, p. 74. 8vo. 1747. Southerne's acknowledgments to her in his Life in the *General Dictionary*; and Burnet's character of her in the Vol. x. in the account of Mrs. Wharton. Lord Lansdowne has a poem on her.

As to Mrs. Behn's character, it is allowed that she was of a capacity above most of her sex who have obliged the public. She had a ready command of pertinent expressions, and was of a fancy pregnant and fluent : whence it is that she wrote with a facility, spirit, and warmth, especially in amorous subjects, superior to every other poetess of the age, and many of the poets too ; so that none among us may, perhaps, more justly be called the ENGLISH SAPPHO, equalling her either for description, or perhaps experience, in the flames of love, and excelling in her personal temptation to it; being a graceful comely woman, with brown hair, and a piercing eye, as one picture represents her — whether the same painted by Mr. Riley I am not positive.[4] I am told, moreover, by one who knew her, that she had a happy vein in determining any disputes or controversies that might arise in company ; having such agreeable repartees at hand upon all occasions, and so much discretion in the timing of them, that she played them off like winning cards. Mrs. Behn was between forty and fifty years of age at the time of her death, which was hastened by an injudicious physician.

John Downes, the prompter, in his *Roscius Anglicanus*, 8vo. 1708, says, Mrs. Behn wrote also *The Jealous Bridegroom* about 1672, a good play, which lasted six nights ; and that Mr. Otway first

---

[4] Pope has the following couplet on her dramatic writings : —

> "The stage how loosely does Astrea tread,
> Who fairly puts all characters to bed."

F

tried to act on the stage the King's part in this
play, but the great audience dashed him and
spoiled him for an actor; and that Nat. Lee having the same fate in acting Duncan in *Macbeth*,
ruined him for a performer also, and from that
time their genius set them upon poetry.

Old Mr. John Bowman, the player, told me that
Mrs. Behn was the first person he ever knew or
heard of, who made the liquor called Milk Punch.

Langbaine, in his notice of Mrs. Behn's tragi-
comedy *Widow Ranter, or the History of Bacon
in Virginia,* 1690, remarks " For the story of Bacon I know no history that relates it; but his
catastrophe is founded on the known story of
Cassius, who perished by the hand of his freed-
man Dandorus, believing his friend Brutus van-
quished." Oldys adds, " There was an insurrec-
tion in Virginia a little before, made by one
Nathaniel Bacon, a great opposer of the royal
party there, in conjunction with one Drummond
a Scot, and among others.[5] Bacon died there in
1675, as near as I can compute, or 1676, as others;
and his accomplices being routed and subdued by
the royal party, thirteen of them were hanged,
some say eighteen.' There were two or three
pamphlets published on the subject, one called
' *Strange News from Virginia;* being a relation
of all occurrences in that Country since the
Death of Nathaniel Bacon: with an Account of
thirteen persons tried and executed for their Rebellion there, 4to. 1676.' The account in this
pamphlet is extracted from a letter written by
Sir John Burrey, the admiral who transported
some soldiers thither. He arrived there on the
29th of January, and says that Bacon had been

---

[5] The whole of the narrative connected with this affair
of Bacon is preserved in one thick volume in Her Majesty's State Paper Office, London. There are besides, in
the same office, a variety of scattered papers relative to
the same subject.

dead two months before. Query, if the Bacon
before mentioned was not that Nat. Bacon of
Gray's Inn [6], who in 1647 and 1651, published
his two volumes, 4to. of *The Historical Discourse
on the Government of England*, in which he was
blackened. It has been twice reprinted in folio;
and it is said Mr. Selden assisted him in it; but
I think that does not evidently appear. See
Bishop Nicolson's descriptive character of this
book [*English Hist. Library*, p. 193., ed. 1736.]
Old Mr. Nathaniel Booth of Gray's Inn has assured me, that this Nathaniel Bacon did go over
to Virginia; but he could not remember what he
had heard he did there. See more in my Catalogue of English Lives, fol., in the notes, &c." [7]

ELDERTON. — This Elderton was a famous comedian, who flourished about 1570; a facetious
fuddling companion, who, having a great readi-
ness at rhyming, composed abundance of sonnets
and catches upon love and wine, which were then
in great vogue among the light and merry part of
the town; but he was not more notable for his
drollery and his doggrel than he was for his drinking, insomuch that he was seldom remembered for
his singular faculty in either of the former, but his
thorough practice in the latter was joined to it.
Wherefore we find him called the Bacchanalian

---

[6] Or his son, for the insurgent is called in *The History
of the American Plantations*, 2 vols. 8vo., Nat. Bacon,
jun. and Col. Bacon, a young sprightly man, who had
been a lawyer too.—*Oldys.*

[7] For biographical notices of Mrs. Behn consult the
History of her Life and Manners, written by One of the
Fair Sex, prefixed to her *Histories and Novels*, 2 vols.
12mo. 1735; Kippis's *Biog. Britannica*; Langbaine's *Account of Dramatic Poets*, p. 17., ed. 1691; Cibber's *Lives
of the Poets*, iii. 17; Freeman's *Kentish Poets*; *Retrospec-
tive Rev.*, 1853, i. 1—18.; Nichols's *Poems*, i. 85.; Geneste's
Hist. of the Stage, ii. 79.; and "N. & Q." 1st S. xi. 184.;
2nd S. viii. 265.; ix. 242.

Buffoon, the red-nosed ballad-maker, and such like. It seems by this excessive habit he indulged himself in, over his strong drink, that he fell a martyr to Sir John Barleycorn, as some of his contemporary writers have hinted. See the controversial writings of Dr. G. Harvey and Thomas Nash. We find he was dead before the year 1592, and Mr. Camden has preserved this epitaph on him : —

> " Hic situs est sitiens, atque ebrius Eldertonus,
> Quid dico, hic situs est ? hic potius sitis est."
>
> Remains, p. 382, 4to. 1614.

Which may be thus rendered or imitated : —

> Dead drunk here Elderton doth lie;
> Dead as he is, he still is dry :
> So of him it may well be said,
> Here he, but not his thirst, is laid.[8]

FABIAN. — Fabian wrote a continuation of his *Chronicle*, probably to his own death, which was in the custody of John Stow, and unprinted in 1600.[9]   Out of this unprinted part, Hackluyt

---

[8] Stow says (*Survey*, p. 217., 4to. 1599) that Elderton was an attorney of the sheriffs' court in the city of London about the year 1570, and quotes some verses which he wrote about that time, on the erection of the new portico with images at Guildhall.   Warton thinks the following lines by Bishop Hall in his *Satires* were levelled at Elderton : —

> " Some drunken rimer thinks his time well spent,
>   If he can live to see his name in print;
>   Who when he once is fleshed to the presse,
>   And sees his handsell have such fair successe,
>   Sung to the wheele, and sung unto the payle,
>   He sends forth thraves of ballads to the sale."

For notices of Elderton, see Ritson's *Bibliographica Poetica*, p. 198., ed. 1802; Warton's *History of English Poetry*, iii. 431., ed. 1840 ; Hall's *Satires*, by Singer, p. 114. ; *Harleian Miscellany*, by Park, x. 266—274. ; and Chappell's *Popular Music of the Olden Time*, i. 88, 89.

[9] Stow, in the collections which he made for his *Survey*, speaks of a Continuation by Fabian himself, as low as the

cites a note of Sebastian Cabot's discoveries, anno
13 Hen. VII.; but the first edition I have seen
continues the History, as I remember, to 1509,
and that was printed in 1533 [10] [2 vols. fol.], and
Fabian died in 1512. Of Fabian, and the editions of his History, see Tyrrell's Preface; Hearne's
Preface to Robert of Gloucester's *Chronicle*, p.
32.; Strype in *Abp. Parker's Life*, p. 235.; and
what I have said in my Fuller's *Worthies*.[1]

MILTON.—Remember my dates of all his works
at the end of his Life by E. Philips; and what I
have observed in Toland's Life of him, and Bayle's
observation on his style. See one of Mist's Journals upon him [Toland] and his *Amintas*, and the
Answer.

---

third year of Henry VIII., "which Boke (he adds) I
have in writen hand." (MS. Harl. 538.) It is not improbable, as Sir Henry Ellis conjectures, that it might
have gone from Stow's Collection to Sir Robert Cotton's.
   [10] The edition of 1533 was the second: the first edition
was printed by Richarde Pynson in 1516. In the Gren-
ville library are two copies of the third edition, 1559.
One of the copies contains the following MS. note: " It
has not, as far as I know, been noticed, that two editions
of this Chronicle were printed in the same year by Kyng-
ston. The present copy contains matter respecting
Queen Elizabeth at p. 566 to the end, which is not to be
found in the copies of usual occurrence." The other copy
[No. II.] appears to agree with the preceding to page 565.
Pages 566 to the end of 571 differ in the relation of the
death of Queen Mary, which in the first is stated to have
taken place on the XVII. of December, 1558, and in this
copy the XVII. of November is named. The former edition terminates with the coronation of Elizabeth on the
15th of January, and the printing of the book is stated
to have been finished on the 26th of April, 1559. The
last event mentioned in this copy is the Queen's riding
to the Parliament on the 8th of May, though the title-
page mentions " Mense Aprilis," as in the former edition.
   [1] A valuable bibliographical account of Fabian's *Chronicle* is prefixed to the quarto edition of 1811, edited by Sir
Henry Ellis.

See my pamphlet containing the castration of his [Milton's ?] History. His own observations on himself. See my *Universal Spectator* on his Spirit of Liberty ; and the pamphlet written against him, called *No Blind Guides*², &c., and the verses in MS. which I found at the end of another old pamphlet, where I have mentioned the Psalm which Milton, or his father, set to music. Peck's *Life and Works, &c.*, 1740. Wm. Benson's erecting of his monument ; settling 1000*l.* for translating his *Paradise Lost* into Latin on young Dobson — the interest while he was doing it, and the principal when done.

Milton's cipher for secret communication, with others used by the republicans under Oliver, I had among the Royal Letters in Clarendon's collections which I redeemed from perdition, and presented to my late noble Lord of Oxford, and they are still preserved in the Harleian library : but God knows how soon that magnificent collection of Manuscripts may undergo the same dispersion as the printed books, which were sold to Tom Osborne my neighbour for less than 13,000*l.*, though the binding only of the least part of them by his Lordship, cost him 18,000*l.*

A Verbal Index to Milton's *Paradise Lost* was published by Mr. Coxeter in 12mo., 1741, printed for Innis and Brown.

Lauder is now writing a book to prove Milton a plagiary. He begun in one of the Magazines. See an answer in *Mag.* Feb. 1749, and Dr. Kirkpatrick in *The Sea Piece*, 8vo., 1750, Preface. See also a pamphlet published against Lauder, called *Miltonomastix.* See also, *Furius: or a Modest Attempt towards an History of the Life and Surprising Exploits of the famous W. L., Critick and Thief-catcher*, 8vo., 1748.³

---

² By Sir Roger L'Estrange, published in 1660.
³ Lauder was discovered to have forged most of his

SUCKLING. — The largest account of Sir John Suckling is in Lloyd's *Memoirs*, being near six pages in folio, and not a dozen lines of solid history. The whole beginning is a chain of hyperboles, and the whole life may serve to feed the eyes with a full meal of words, and leave the mind quite hungry for the subject matter. My account of him much more complete in the quarto volume of Lives, parchment cover. See also the references in my Fuller's *Worthies* and Winstanley. He was patron to Thomas Nabbes, the dramatic poet, who dedicated his comedy, *Covent Garden*, to him, acted in 1632, printed in 4to. 1638. At Theobald's, 19th Dec. 1630, Sir John Suckling of Witham knighted. (Thos. Walkley's *Cat. of Dukes, &c.*, 8vo. 1639.)

Recollect where I have set down the story my Lord Oxford told me he had from Dean Chetwood, who had it from Lord Roscommon, of Sir John Suckling's being robbed of a casket of jewels and gold when he was going to France by his valet, who I think poisoned him, and stuck the blade of a penknife in Sir John's boot to prevent his pursuit of him, and wounded him incurably in the heel besides.[4] It is in one of my pocket-books, white vellum cover—the white journal that is not gilt.

Remember the MS. account I have about Sir John Suckling's being beaten by Mr. Digby his rival.[5] See the lampoon on him in the pamphlets

parallels, or to have taken them from Hog's Latin version of Milton's poem by Dr. Douglas, now [1764] Canon of Windsor.—*Percy*. *Furius* was written by Henderson, a bookseller. ✓

[4] Suckling was robbed by his valet-de-chambre, and putting on his boot in a passionate hurry to pursue the thief, a rusty nail concealed at the bottom of one of them pierced his heel, and brought on a mortification, of which he died.— *Warton on Pope*, ii. 109.

[5] For the particulars of this cudgelling, see the *Strafforde Letters*, 1739, i. 336.

on the Scots' expedition in Morgan's *Phœnix Britannicus.* Query, if it is not in his tragedy *The Sad
One,* that I remarked a passage in ridicule of Ben
Jonson. In *The Tryal of Skill, or New Session
of the Poets,* fol. 1704, Suckling accuses Thomas
Cheek with having murdered his goblins in every
page.

Sir John Suckling has verses before Coryat's
Crudities, 4to., 1611.

A Letter concerning a Married Life, subscribed
John Suckling, London, Nov. 18, 1629, in the
Ashmolean Library, Oxon.

Sir John Suckling's Letter to Mr. Henry Ger-
min, 1640, a manuscript among the Collection of
Poems of Thomas Brotherton of Hey in Lancashire.

An Elegy upon the Death of the Renowned Sir
John Sutlin, 4to., 1642, with another short poem
"To Sir John Sutlin upon Aglaura." First a
bloody tragedy, then by the said Sir John turned
to a comedy. These poems are in one short 4to.,
but to the copy before me is written "Authore
Gulielmo Norris."

See Thomas Stanley's *Poems,* 8vo., 1651, on Sir
John Suckling's *Picture of Poems.* On Sir John
Suckling's Warlike Preparations for the Scottish
War, in Sir John Mennis's *Musarum Deliciæ.*
Also, in Anthony Hammond's *Miscellany of Poems,*
8vo., 1720. Another Poem, pretended to be writ
from France by Sir John Suckling, 4to., 1641.
*The Conversion of Sir John Suckling from a
Papist to a Protestant,* 4to., 1641.[6]

JOHN TRUSSEL. — Both Bishop Nicolson and

---

[6] The best account of Sir John Suckling is in the Life
prefixed to *Selections from his Works,* by the Rev. Alfred
Suckling, 8vo., 1836. The whole of Sir John Suckling's
Works, containing his Poems, Letters, and Plays, were
published several times by Tonson; and in two neat
volumes by T. Davies, 1770.

Dr. Kennet seem very censorious in their account of John Trussel's Description of the City of Winchester, neither of them appearing to have ever seen it; nor even Anthony Wood, from whom their intelligence is derived. For it is a manuscript in the Norfolcian library, and seems not, in a folio volume as it is, too voluminous for the description of such a city, considering there is a preamble on the origin of cities in general also before it.[7]

---

[7] Besides the MS. in the Norfolcian library, Gough (*British Topog.*, i. 387.) states that "in a catalogue of the famous Robert Smith's books, sold by auction 1682, No. 24., was a MS. entitled 'A Description of the City of Winchester, with an historical relation of divers memorable occurrences touching the same; and prefixed to it, a preamble of the original of Cities in general, by J. Trussel,' fol., which was purchased by a Mr. Rothwell." This MS., written by Trussel about 1620, was in the library of John Duthy, Esq., who permitted Dr. Milner to make extracts from it for his *History and Antiquities of Winchester*, 4to., 1801.

LONDON LIBRARIES.

[The following interesting notices of the London Libraries at the commencement of the last century must be considered as the joint-production of John Bagford and William Oldys — names dear to every literary antiquary. At the death of William Oldys on the 15th of April, 1761, his printed books and manuscripts were purchased by Thomas Davies the bookseller, in whose Catalogue of April 12, 1762, this manuscript is entered as No. 3613, and entitled, " Of London Libraries: with Anecdotes of Collectors of Books, Remarks on Booksellers, and on the first Publishers of Catalogues," 4to. That a work bearing so alluring a title from the pen of William Oldys should awaken the curiosity of bibliographers is what might be expected. Mr. Bolton Corney informs us, that " Mr. Heber, whose copy of [Davies's] Catalogue of 1762 lies before me, has marked this article with *N.B. N.B.* It evidently set him on the *qui vive*." (*Curiosities of Literature Illustrated*, second edition, p. 169.) Mr. John Fry, too, in a note to this article copied from Davies's Catalogue, in his *Bibliographical Memoranda*, 4to. 1816, p. 37., adds, "This must be a curious article; *Query*. In whose possession is it ? "

The manuscript now before us, however, does not fully correspond in contents with those set forth in the title-page advertised by Davies, as the last two topics are unnoticed ; so that we may have only a portion of a larger work left incomplete by our assiduous antiquary. Nevertheless, in the account of the London Libraries now presented to our readers, Oldys has thrown open, not merely " to students and curious persons," as the charter of the British Museum has it, but to the public at large, the inexhaus-

tible treasures contained within them, and as such his
work will be acceptable to every student engaged in biographical and historical researches.

The history of this literary relic is soon told. It was
commenced by the ingenious John Bagford, whose first
rough and incomplete draft is among his Collectanea in the
Harl. MS. 5900, fol. 44., and was printed in *The Monthly
Miscellany, or Memoirs for the Curious*, ii. 167., 4to., 1708.
Bagford died at Islington on May 15, 1716, aged sixty-
five. Oldys availed himself of the fugitive collections of
this industrious bookseller, or rather book-broker, and
from his extensive acquaintance with the literary treasures of the metropolis, was better qualified to carry out
the object proposed by his more humble precursor. Dr.
William Hunter became the fortunate possessor of Oldys's
manuscript, as it was discovered in his Museum, now
belonging to the University of Glasgow. We are indebted to the kindness of His Grace the Duke of Argyle
for securing us the opportunity of giving it publicity;
as also to the Rev. Principal Barclay for his assistance,
and to the Curator of the Museum, Dr. Rogers: the
latter gentleman having been at considerable pains to
procure us a Transcript of the MS., and then adding to
his kindness by collating it with the original.]

The learned and ingenious men of all countries
are apt to inquire wherever they go after the repositories of learning and ingenuity; and not only
content themselves with what they moot of it
among the living, but must be satisfied also with
what testimonies thereof has been left by the
dead.

Yet foreign nations have the art of representing
more considerably their treasures of this kind
than we have, and indeed they appear so to the
eye, though, setting aside the greater pomp and
parade of their books, England may produce as
many that are learnedly and solidly written, perhaps as that magazine of arts may, Rome itself.

London and Westminster are well stored not

only with printed books, but manuscript records, and other muniments of great antiquity, besides statues, models, paintings, and all other curiosities both in Art and Nature, though we are not so ostentatious, as I said, of them,—have not the talent of magnifying them so much as some of our neighbours have.

TOWER OF LONDON.—Of our Public Records in the Tower, those which are particularly in Wakefield Tower, are in great number, and well worth the inspection of the curious. They have of late had a due regard paid to them ; have been now modelled and digested, and reposited in cases.[1] In the White Tower are vast number of records relating to Monasteries, &c., several letters of Kings, Princes, Dukes, &c., from several parts of the world, as Tartary, Barbary, Spain, France, Italy, &c., to our Kings in England, also restored very conveniently to order and method. The building itself was a chapel of the palace, and is a very uncommon sort of structure, and by the late Queen's liberality rendered both useful and ornamental.

CHAPTER HOUSE, WESTMINSTER.—In the Exchequer at Westminster, the Records were lately in the custody of the Lord Treasurer. There are the two most ancient books in this kingdom, made in William the Conqueror's time, called the *Doomsday Books*; the one in quarto containing the Description or Survey of Essex, Norfolk, and Suffolk ; the other, in folio, being the same for all the shires in England, from Cornwall to the River

---

[1] In 1703, Queen Anne appointed that proper care should be taken to provide a convenient and safe place for depositing all the Records in this Tower, and a sufficient number of clerks to clean, sort, digest, &c., the same, under the inspection of William Petyt, Esq.

Tyne, well worth the notice.[2] There are also many other ancient and rare Records, as Powell in his *Repertory* [3], Prynne, Cotton, and above all, the seventeen volumes of Rymer's *Fœdera*, sufficiently evidence.[4]

The Parliament Rolls are in an old stone tower in the Old Palace Yard, Westminster, and the Papers of State, from the beginning of Henry VIII. to this time, are kept in the fine built gate as you go through to the Cockpit, and is called the

---

[2] A very carefully-executed lithographic facsimile of so much of *Domesday Book* as relates to the county of *Kent* is in the course of preparation by Mr. Netherclift. It will be accompanied by a translation and illustrative notes by the Rev. L. B. Larking, from whose vast knowledge of all that relates to the History of Kent, much valuable light will assuredly be thrown upon the nature of this invaluable national record. That portion which relates to *Cornwall* has lately been copied and printed by photozincography by Colonel Sir Henry James, R.E., by order of Her Majesty's Government; and may be procured of any bookseller for a few shillings.

[3] "Repository of Records remaining in the Four Treasuries on the Receipt side at Westminster, the two Remembrancers of the Exchequer; with a Brief Introductory Index of the Records in the Chancery and Tower; in which is contained whatsoever may give satisfaction to the searcher for tenure or title in anything." By Robert Powell. London, 1634, 4to. Rymer's *Fœdera*, edited by George Holmes, makes 20 vols. fol. 1727—1735.

[4] The Chapter House is situated on the south-east side of Westminster Abbey, immediately adjoining the entrance to Poets' Corner. It contained muniments of the most valuable, but miscellaneous nature. In 1807, the Record Commission ordered an Inventory to be made of them. Three copies only were taken of it; one of them, with coloured drawings of the building, is at the British Museum, Addit. MS. 8977. Sir Harris Nicolas made an abstract of the Alphabetical Index, which be printed in the *Gent. Mag.* for Feb. 1830, p. 118. See also Thomas's *Hand-Book of the Records*, pp. 287-297. The documents have recently been transferred to the Rolls Office, Chancery Lane.

G

Paper Office. It was built by Henry VIII., and is one of the most curious pieces of workmanship in Europe for flint work, and it is reported that Hans Holbein was the architect.[5] Dr. Forbes is now collecting all the State Papers here relating to the reign of Queen Elizabeth, in order to publish them in several volumes in folio.[6]

COTTONIAN LIBRARY.—Sir Robert Cotton's Library of Manuscripts, founded by himself,the fruits of forty years' inquiry, expense, interest, and assistance, bequeathed through Act of Parliament for the public benefit. They are gathered into about 1000 great volumes, and reposited in fourteen wainscot presses under the distinction of the twelve Cæsars, and of Cleopatra and Faustina. They are now in Lord Ashburnham's house[7] by the

---

[5] For views of Holbein's gate, Whitehall, see *Vetusta Monumenta; Londina Illustrata;* Smith's *Westminster;* and Dodsley's *London.* When Strype drew up his additions to Stow, the uppermost room, in Holbein's gateway, was used as the State Paper Office. (Book vi. p. 5.)

[6] *A Full View of the Public Transactions in the Reign of Queen Elizabeth.* By Patrick Forbes, M.D. Lond. 1740-1., fol. 2 vols. A series of letters and other papers of state, written by Queen Elizabeth and her principal ministers, and by the foreign princes and ministers with whom she had negociations, illustrated with facsimile autographs. Are these the earliest *facsimiles* published in England? See Ayscough's *Catalogue,* p. 99., for a list of Dr. Forbes's papers in the British Museum.

[7] The Cottonian library was deposited in Ashburnham House in 1730. On the 23rd Oct. 1731, a fire broke out and consumed a portion of the collection. The MSS. of the Royal and Cottonian libraries at this time were in the same room above the one where the fire commenced. At the first alarm, Mr. Casley took care to remove the famous Alexandrian MS. in the Royal Collection, and now in the British Museum, Royal MS. 1 D. v.—viii. 4to. From "A Report of the Committee appointed to View the Cottonian Library," Lond. 1732, fol., it appears that " the number of manuscript volumes contained in the library before the fire was 958; of which are lost, burnt, or

Abbey at Westminster, and ten rings of MSS. in same room with them, as his library of printed books are in the next, whereof Dr. Bentley [8] is keeper at the salary of 200*l.* per an., and Mr. Casley [9] under-keeper. This Cottonian library has been, and not improperly, called the English Vatican, though the Pope's conclave made some endeavours, after the foundation, 1631 [10], to incorporate it with that of Rome. It is the grand repository to which our Antiquaries and Historians have had access, to their great improvement and elucidation, and the facility of this access has greatly advanced the credit and use of it.

> " Omnis ab illo
> Et Camdene tua, et Seldeni gloria crevit." [1]
> [" Camden to him, to him doth Selden, owe
> Their glory: what they got from him did grow."]

---

entirely spoiled, 114; and damaged 98: so that the said library, at present, consists of 746 entire volumes, and 68 defective ones." Mr. Sims, in his *Hand-Book to the Library of the British Museum*, states, that "since 1842 one hundred volumes written upon vellum, and ninety-seven upon paper, have been restored under the directions of Sir Frederic Madden."

[8] Dr. Richard Bentley, the celebrated critic and classic of Phalaris celebrity, succeeded Mr. Justel as Keeper of the Royal Library at St. James's on Dec. 23, 1693. Ob. July 14, 1742. In Addit. MS. 4696. (Brit. Mus.) is a Schedule of all the MSS., parchments, written records, and other memorials, and of the coins, medals, and other rarities contained in the Cottonian library, made by Dr. Richard Bentley the 10th of May, 1718.

[9] Mr. David Casley drew up "A Catalogue of the Manuscripts of the King's Library; an Appendix to the Catalogue of the Cottonian Library, together with an Account of Books burnt or damaged by a late fire," &c. Lond. 1734, 4to.

[10] Sir Robert Cotton commenced his splendid collection in 1588; was knighted 1603; created a baronet 1611; and died in May, 1631, his death being hastened by the loss of his library, which had been twice taken possession of by government.

[1] Weever's *Funeral Monuments*, Preface.

It consists of ancient MSS. in Divinity, History, and especially relating to English History, ecclesiastical and civil: "in so much, that the fountains have been fain to fetch water from the stream," says Fuller; "and the secretaries of state and clerks of the council glad from hence to borrow back again many originals which, being lost by casualty or negligence of officers, had been neglected" to be recovered to their proper repositories when some danger of fire or necessity of repairs, &c., I have heard, had removed them for protection to this known preserver of such instructive curiosities, with many ancient Saxon Charters, coins, &c.[2]

In the drawers are many choice Roman antiquities not mentioned in Dr. Smith's *Catalogue*[3]: as a brass image, fibulas, lamps, rings, seals, weapons, and other great rarities, taken notice of by very few who have seen that place. There are many old reliques which belonged to the Monasteries here in England before the Dissolution. Amongst others, the claw of a griffin with a silver hoop, on the great end of it a Saxon inscription; but I take it rather to be the horn of some animal. There is an old painted altar that belonged to the Monastery of Great Saint Bartholomew, London; some pictures of the Kings of England (also of Camden, Spelman, Attwood, Ben Jonson, &c.) on

---

[2] Vide Nicolson's Preface to Part III. of his *Historical Libraries*; Letters of *Journey through England* [by Paul Hentzner, ed. 1757, p. 30.]; Fuller's *Worthies*; *Life of Sir Robert Cotton* [by Dr. Thomas Smith?]; and *The Present State of the Cotton Library* [fol. 1732.].—*Oldys*.

[3] Dr. Thomas Smith, Fellow of Magdalen College, Oxford, compiled a Catalogue of this library, entitled "Catalogus Librorum MSS. Bibliothecæ Cottonianæ, etc. Scriptore Thoma Smitho, Eccles. Anglicanæ Presbytero." Oxon. 1696, fol. It is valuable as affording a clue to the identification of the burnt manuscripts. The Catalogue at present in use was prepared by Joseph Planta, Esq., fol. 1802.

board, the oldest I have seen. There is a large book with several excellent designs for the Entrance of Henry VIII.[4] I shall leave the description of these most excellent MSS., as to their antiquity, illuminations, curious writing, purport, &c., to a more able performer. Had the late Mr. Humphrey Wanley[5] had encouragement, he could have exhibited this library to the world with as much advantages as Lambecius has done the Emperor's at Vienna.[6] The ancient Genesis there deserves a particular description.[7] It is in all probability one of the rarest manuscripts in the world, and as old as any : it is in Greek capitals with figures, and well worthy the regard of the most curious. The place where those jewels were reposited, before the last removal, is the remaining part of the palace of St. Edward, the King; and one of the oldest structures of those times.[8]

---

[4] " Designs for interviews in the time of Henry VIII." — *Bagford's MS.*

[5] In the year 1701, Humphrey Wanley, Matthew Hutton, and John Anstis, three eminent antiquaries, were appointed to examine carefully into the state of the Cottonian Library. Their report, dated June 22, 1703, is extant in manuscript, prefixed to a copy of Dr. Thomas Smith's *Catalogue of the Cott. MSS.* in the King's library at the British Museum, which also contains Wanley's MS. Catalogue of the Charters in the Cottonian collection.

[6] Peter Lambecius, a learned bibliographer, was born in 1628, and died in 1680. His great Catalogue of the imperial library was published in 8 vols. fol. from 1665 to 1679, under the title of *Commentariorum de augustissima Bibliotheca Cæsarea Vindobonensi,* libri octo.

[7] The invaluable MS. of the Greek Genesis (Cotton. MS. Otho, B. vi.), written upon vellum in the fourth century, with miniatures, was supposed to have been irrecoverably damaged by the fire at Ashburnham House; but has since been restored under the directions of Sir Frederic Madden.

[8] This last sentence was written by Bagford, but slightly altered, and that incorrectly, by Oldys. Cotton House, near the west end of Westminster Hall (the place alluded to) was sold to the Crown in the reign of Queen

G 3

WESTMINSTER ABBEY LIBRARY. — In the great cloister of the abbey is a well-furnished library, considering the time when it was erected by Dr. Williams, Dean of Westminster and Bishop of Lincoln; who was a great promoter of learning. He purchased the books of the heirs of one Baker of Highgate, and founded it for public use every day in Term, from nine to twelve in the forenoon, and from two till four in the afternoon. The MSS. are kept in the inner part, but by an accident many of them were burnt. There I saw that pompous and rare book of the Rules and Ceremonies of the Coronation of our Kings of England. There is a MS. Catalogue of the books in the library.[9] In the room called the Museum,

---

Anne for 4500*l.*, by Sir John Cotton, the great-grandson of the founder of the library. In 1712, the library was removed to Essex House in the Strand, and again in 1730, to Ashburnham House; the following year to the old Dormitory of Westminster School; and eventually transferred in 1753 to the British Museum.

[9] There was also a library belonging to the King's palace at Westminster, as appears from an order in Council in the reign of Edward VI. for "purging the library of Westminster of all missals, legends, and other superstitious volumes, and delivering their garniture to Sir Anthony Aucher." (Collier's *Eccles. Hist.* ii. 307., fol.) Dean Williams converted a waste room, situate in the east side of the cloisters, into a library; which he enriched with the valuable works from the collection of Sir Richard Baker, author of *The Chronicles of the Kings of England,* which cost him 500*l.* A Catalogue of this library is in Harl. MS. 694. There is also a MS. Catalogue, compiled in 1798 by Dr. Dakin, the precentor, arranged alphabetically. See Botfield's *Cathedral Libraries of England,* pp. 430—464.; and an interesting paper on this library by W. H. Hart, Esq., F.S.A., read at the meeting of the London and Middlesex Archæological Society, Oct. 25, 1860, and printed in the *Gent. Mag* for March, 1861, p. 239. It is scarcely necessary to remind our readers of the admirable description of this library given by Washington Irving in his *Sketch Book.*

at Westminster, is a collection of books given by Dr. Busby for the use of the scholars.[1]

OLD ROYAL LIBRARY. — St. James's Library was founded by King Henry VIII., is well furnished with choice books collected by John Leland, and others at the Dissolution of the Abbeys. There is a great quantity of books that were first printed, both on vellum and paper, in all languages. The Catalogue of the MSS. is printed in the General Catalogue of Manuscripts in England.[2] This library was founded for the use of the Princes of the Blood, as Prince Edward; and our Kings besides, had several studios and libraries at several places; as Whitehall, Hampton Court, Nonsuch, Windsor, Oatlands, Greenwich, &c. ; but this at St. James's was the chief, and hath been used and highly esteemed by the learned in all times. The keeping of it hath from time to time, in the several reigns, been by Leland, Delayne, Traherne[3], Ascham, Patrick Young (Patricius Junius), and now in the keeping of Dr. Bentley. It would redound much to our reputation that foreigners were better acquainted with it.

ARTILLERY GROUND (West.) There was formerly a piece of ground taken in and walled not far from St. James's, near Leicester Fields, by the

---

[1] The "Museum" is now called the Library at Westminster School. It consists principally of old editions of the Classics. Many Oriental Books were added about Warren Hastings' time. The most recent bequests made to it were by the late Sir Everard Home, the eminent surgeon, and the late Dr. Bull, Canon of Christ Church, Oxford.

[2] " Catalogus Lib. MSS. Angliæ et Hiberniæ in unum collecti, cum Indice Alphabetico," fol. Oxon. 1697. An account of the old Royal library is given in Birch's Life of Prince Henry, ed. 1760, pp. 161—166.

[3] Delayne and Traherne are omitted in Mr. Edwards's list of Royal librarians in his Memoirs of Libraries, i. 424.

procurement of Prince Henry for the exercise of
arms, which he much delighted in ; and there was
a house built at one end of it for an armory, and
a well-furnished library of all sorts of books relating to Feats of Arms, Chivalry, Military Affairs,
Encamping, Fortification, the best that could be
collected of that kind, and in all languages, at the
cost and charge of that Prince, who had a learned
librarian, whose name I have forgot. It was
called the Artillery Ground, and continued till the
Restoration of King Charles II., and then fell into
the hands of Lord Gerard, who let the ground out
to build upon about the year 1677.[4]

ABP. TENISON'S LIBRARY. — In the churchyard
of St. Martin's in the Fields Dr. Thomas Tenison, then rector of that parish, but since Archbishop of Canterbury, built a noble structure,
extremely well contrived for the placing of the
books and lights. It was begun and finished in
the year 1684, and by him well furnished with the
best modern books in most faculties. There any
student may repair, and has liberty of making
what researches he pleases, first giving in his name
and place of abode.[5]

---

[4] The western Artillery Ground is better known by the
name of the Military Garden. "On the west side of
Lord Newport's garden (where Gerard Street, &c., are
now situate) was a Military, or Artillery Ground, wherein
were exercised the militia of Middlesex, and trained
bands of Westminster." (Maitland's *London*, p. 1335.)
"Where Gerard Street is, was an Artillery Ground, or
Military Garden, made by Prince Henry." (Walpole,
ed. Dallaway, v. 60.) The library connected with this
Armory was doubtless incorporated with the old Royal
Library at St. James's, as we are informed by Mr. Thomas
Watts, the Assistant Keeper of the Printed Books at the
British Museum, that many of Prince Henry's volumes relating to military matters are now in the national library.
[5] Abp. Tenison's library was in Castle Street, St. Mar-
tin's Lane, immediately behind the National Gallery, and
was open to the parishioners of St. Martin's-in-the-Fields ;

LAMBETH LIBRARY. — At Lambeth Palace over the Cloyster is a well furnished library. The oldest of the books were Dudley's, Earl of Leicester, which from time to time have been augmented by several archbishops of that see. It had a great loss in being deprived of Archbishop Sheldon's admirable Collection of Missals, Breviaries, Primers, &c., relating to the service of the church, as also Abp. Sancroft's.[6] There is another apartment for MSS., not only belonging to the see, but those of the Lord Carew [George, Earl of Totness,] who had been Deputy of Ireland, many of them relating to the state and history of that kingdom.[7]

GRAY'S INN hath a library for the use of the students of that society, most of them relating to

---

St. James's, Westminster; St. Anne's, Soho; and St. George's, Hanover Square. For particulars of it, see Evelyn's *Diary*, 15th Feb. 1683-4 ; and *Report of Public Libraries*, 1849, p. 64. It was dispersed by auction in the month of June, 1861.

[6] Abp. Sancroft's valuable collection of books and MSS. had actually been placed in the archiepiscopal library ; but owing to his deprivation, he eventually presented them to Emmanuel College, Cambridge, of which he was Master from 1662 to 1665.

[7] When the archiepiscopal library occupied those old galleries above the cloisters, the want of warmth and comfort was such an infliction, that the late Sir Harris Nicolas was wont to say, that in winter none but Captain Parry or his crew could possibly make use of the collection. It is now lodged and admirably arranged in the noble hall, built or restored by Archbishop Juxon. An elaborate catalogue of the tracts in this library was drawn up by Dr. Ducarel, in 3 vols. fol. 1773. The Rev. H. J. Todd drew up one of the manuscripts, 1812 ; and the Rev. Dr. Maitland published two lists of its Early Printed Books in 1843 and 1845, 8vo. For an account of this library and its early librarians, see Ducarel's *History of Lambeth Palace*, 4to. 1785, pp. 47-70. ; also Botfield's *Cathedral Libraries of England*, pp. 189-258.

the laws and history of this kingdom; first founded by the Lord Verulam.

LINCOLN's INN hath a good library of law, much augmented by that of the Lord Chief Justice Hale, amongst which are many MSS. of his own writing.[8]

THE TWO TEMPLES have each a library. The Lord Chief Justice Coke gave most if not all his excellent MSS. of Law and History to the Inner Temple. The Middle Temple is frequently resorted to. Walter Williams, Esq., was the keeper about twenty years ago.[9]

CORPORATION LIBRARY. — In the Guild Hall of the City of London is the Treasury of their Records, Charters, Laws, Privileges, Acts of Common Council, their Paper Book in the Chamberlain's Office, some very ancient, and most of them

---

[8] Lincoln's Inn library is the oldest in London, it dates from 1497, when John Nethersale made a bequest towards the building of a library for the benefit of the students of the laws of England. The present library was opened Oct. 30, 1845, and is 80 feet long, 40 feet wide, and 44 feet high. A Catalogue of the Printed Books, to which is prefixed a Short Account of the MSS. was published in 1835. A Catalogue of the MSS. was compiled, in 1837, by Mr. Hunter; and another of the printed books by Mr. W. H. Spilsbury, the librarian, in 1859.

[9] The library of the Middle Temple was founded by Robert Ashley, Esq. by Will, dated 27 Sept. 1641. Three Catalogues have been printed: 1. Catalogus Librorum Bibliothecæ Honorabilis Societatis Medii Templi Londini. Impressa. Anno. Dom. 1734. Carolo Worsley, Armigero Thesaurario Existente, 4to. 2. Catalogus Continens, Additi Fuerunt, ab Anno 1734, ad hoc tempus. Impress. Anno Dom. 1766. Prehonorabili Thoma Sewell, Milite, Scriniorum sacrorum Magistro, Thesaurario existente, 4to. 3. Bibliotheca Illustris Medii Templi Societatis in Ordinem juxtà rerum naturam redacta ac digesta: V. Iduum Sept. M.DCC. Auspicio et Sumptu Burth. Shower, Militis, Hujus Ædis Quæstoris. Lond. 1700, 8vo.

are in the custody of their Town Clerk; there
are great variety, and worthy the sight of the
curious.[1]

In the days of King Edward VI., in the chapel
called the Lord Mayor's Chapel adjoining to
Guild Hall, was a large library all of manuscripts.
They were borrowed with an intent never to be
returned by the Duke of Somerset to furnish his
study in his pompous house in the Strand. They
are reported to have been five [three ?] cart
loads.[2] I mention this to note that the city had
then a Public Library besides others that were
within the walls, as at the Greyfriars in Newgate
Street, now called Christ Church, containing a
great number of manuscripts of which Sir Richard
Whittington was the chief donor, at a great expense, no doubt, seeing we are informed by Clement Reyner, of the great sum which a manuscript
of Lyra cost that worthy citizen.[3]

---

[1] These charters, records, &c., are still in the custody
of the Town Clerk.
[2] The ancient library, founded by Sir Richard Whittington in the fifteenth century, was of some extent and
importance, as is shown by the will of John Carpenter,
Town Clerk, which directs some of his books to be placed
in the Common Library at Guildhall for the profit of the
students there, and those discoursing to the common people. In the records of the corporation is a petition of
John Clipstone, the librarian, in the reign of Henry VI.,
to the Mayor and Aldermen, in which he speaks of the
great attendance and charge of the library.—Mr. W. H.
Overall's paper in the *London and Middlesex Archæological Transactions*, vol. i. p. 352.
[3] The most considerable Franciscan collection of books
seems to have been at the London monastery on the site
of Christ Hospital, Newgate Street, for which the first
stone of a new building was laid by Sir Richard Whittington on the 21st Oct. 1421. After it was completed
100 marks were expended on a transcript of the works of
Nicholas de Lira, to be chained in the library. Stow's
Survey by Strype, book iii. 130. Whittington's library
was a handsome room, 129 feet long, and 31 feet broad,

The White Friars spared for no cost to procure books, and their Collection must be large and choice. Bishop Bale, one of their fraternity, says that no book was to be sold but they had their emissaries to buy it. The Carmelites engrossed all the books they could lay their hands on, and it is probable all the other Orders did the like. So that a layman, though he had both money and learning, would have but few come to his hands, wherefore books and learning were seldom met with out of a monastery.

Sion College was founded by Dr. White, Vicar of St. Dunstan's in the West, in the year 16 ... [1623], for the use of divines and others in and about London ; they are a body corporate. Great part of their library was destroyed by the fire in 1666 ; but some of the books were saved by the vigilance of the librarian.   Since it hath been rebuilt, and the library plentifully supplied with good books by the bounty of the Lord Berkeley [4], and of late by Sir Philip Sydenham, [Bart. of Brympton in Somersetshire.]   It is a most convenient place for situation, out of the noise of coaches, and the only public library within the walls of the city : a large spacious room, very convenient, and capable of receiving many thousand volumes to fill up the stands.   There should be a complete collection of bibles and of good historians ; but benefactors too often bestow on public libraries books of little value, such as come cheapest or most casually to them.   It has now a good, industrious librarian, Mr. Wm. Reading, who, observing there had not been a Catalogue printed since the fire, though the collection has been considerably augmented by the addition of

wainscoted throughout, and fitted with shelves neatly carved, with desks and settles. It formed the northern side of the quadrangle.
   [4] George, first Earl of Berkeley, obit. 1698.

four entire libraries, as well as by inferior bene-
factions, and the annual contributions of Stationers' Hall, and it having been publicly observed
by the Governors of the said college on his behalf,
that by reason of the narrowness of his salary, and a
heavy debt which has lain upon the college ever
since the rebuilding it after the aforesaid casualty,
there was no means to print a Catalogue, and
make him some moderate recompense for his labour therein; but by the assistance of about two
hundred subscribers advancing a guinea a-piece,
with the payment of another upon receipt of the
book, he did therefore publish Proposals to that
effect in Nov. 1721, and the catalogue is now
printed in a handsome folio volume, introduced
with an account of the ancient and present state
of the said college and library.[5]

---

[5] Sion College was founded by Letters Patent granted
by Charles I. in 1630, in conformity with the provisions
of the Will of the Rev. Thomas White, D.D. Canon of
Christ Church, and Vicar of St. Dunstan's in the West,
who died in 1623. The library was founded a few years
later by the Rev. John Simpson, one of Dr. White's exe-
cutors. A copy of every book entered at Stationers'
Hall was given to this library by Acts 8 Anne and 54
Geo. III.; but in 1836 this privilege was taken away by
the Act 6 & 7 Will. IV. c. 110, and a compensation
awarded of 363*l.* 15*s.* 2*d.* payable annually from the Treasury. The first catalogue of this library is entitled " Catalogus Universalia Librorvm omnium in Bibliotheca
Collegii Sionii apud Londinenses. Vna cum Elencho
Interpretūm S. S. Scripturæ, Casuistarum, Theologorum
Scholasticorum, &c. Omnia per J. S. [J. Spencer] Biblio-
thecarium (quanta potuit diligentia) ordine Alphabetico ·
disposita, in unam collecta et propriis sumptibus in Stu-
diosorum usum excusa. Lond. Ex Officina Typog. Rob.
Leybourni, 1650, 4to." " An Account of the London
Clergy's Library in Sion College," by Wm. Reading, is
appended to his *Bibliothecæ Cleri Londinensis in Collegio
Sionensi Catalogus.* Lond. 1724, fol. The library at present contains about 50,000 volumes. *An Account of
Sion College,* consisting of documents elucidating its his-

H

St. Paul's School. — There are other small libraries within the city walls, as that of St. Paul's School, first founded by Dean Colet, and since rebuilt by the Company of Mercers. The founder left them many good books, both in MS. and print, mostly Grammatical in Hebrew, Greek, and Latin; they were destroyed in the Great Fire, with Mr. Cromleholme's, the Upper Master of the said school, which was a curious collection of the best impressions and editions of the Classics, neatly bound, the best private collection then about London.[6] He was a great lover of his books, and the loss of them hastened the loss of his life. Since then they have been supplied by all sorts of Lexicons, Dictionaries, and Grammars, in Hebrew, Chaldee, Greek, and Latin for the use of the Upper Scholars, and with many other books of more general matter and use.[7]

In 1707, the Dean and Chapter of St. Paul's purchased the library of Mr. Gery, Vicar of St. Mary's, Islington, for 500l., one moiety the gift of Dr. Stanley — a good beginning for a future foundation.

Heralds' Office. — In the Heralds' Office is a curious collection of books relating to Heraldry, Arms, Descents, Dignities, and Precedences, Solemnities, Processions, Coronations, Marriages, Christenings, Visitations of Counties, Obits, and Funerals. In the time of the civil confusions they

---

tory to the present time, has lately been printed for the use of the Fellows.

[6] Samuel Cromleholme was head-master 1657 to 1671. He was the tutor of some remarkable men, such as the great Duke of Marlborough, Bishop Cumberland, Mr. Dodington, Dr. Gower, and the Rev. John Strype.

[7] A list of the benefactors to the library of St. Paul's School, together with a Catalogue of the books, will be found in Knight's *Life of Dr. John Colet*, pp. 437. 475., edit. 1724.

lost many, which fell into the hands of some who wanted the honesty to restore them. There has been since some reparation made by the Earl of Arundel's Collections the noble present of the Duke of Norfolk, whereof a Catalogue was printed in 4to. 1681.[8] Also by those which had been of Vincent's collection, and bought by Ralph Sheldon, Esq., of Weston, in Warwickshire, who gave them to the office[9]; besides the libraries of those valuable memorials in the particular hands of the several heralds of the said office, as Sir Harry St. George, more particularly of this about 350 vols. fol., and Mr. Le Neve, the latter of whom dying on the 24th Sept. 1729, bequeathed his vast treasure of Historical Antiquities, consisting of about 2000 printed books, and above 1200 MSS. interspersed with many notes of his own, to a namesake who was no relation to him,

---

[8] Evelyn, in his *Diary*, Aug. 29, 1678, says, "I was called to London to wait upon the Duke of Norfolk, who having at my sole request bestowed the Arundelian library on the Royal Society, sent to me to take charge of the books, only stipulating that I would suffer the Heralds' chief officer, Sir William Dugdale, to have such of them as concerned heraldry and the Marshal's office, books of armory and genealogies, the Duke being Earl Marshal of England." See more respecting this gift in Nichols's *Illustrations*, iv. 63–66. The Catalogue is entitled, "Bibliotheca Norfolciana; sive Catalogus librorum Manuscriptorum et impressorum, quos Henricus Howard, Dux Norfolciæ, Regiæ Societati Londinensi, pro scientiâ naturali promovendâ donavit, ordine alphabetico dispositus. 4to. Londini, 1681." A Catalogue of the Arundel MSS. given to the College of Arms was drawn up in 1829 by Mr. W. H. Black, with a Preface by Sir Charles George Young, the present Garter King of Arms, by whom it was privately printed.

[9] Augustine Vincent, Windsor herald, died Jan. 11, 1625–6. His son John, although a good genealogist, herald, and antiquary, was so fond of liquor, that he pawned some of his father's literary labours to pay tavern bills. He disposed of 240 MSS. to Ralph Sheldon, Esq., who bequeathed them to the College of Arms. — *Noble.*

H 2

nor had any curiosity in them, so they were sold
in Covent Garden about ——.[1]

There was a catalogue of the books in the library at the College of Arms in London, collected
by Peter Le Neve, Esq., Norroy, a transcript of
which by Chas. Mawson in MS. fol. was in Sclater Bacon's library. About a year and a half
after the death of Mr. Le Neve his books were
sold by auction, and what that antiquary had
been his whole life in getting together were scattered again in two months. Not that I would
quarrel with auctions; they certainly are, for the
generality, of great convenience to the learned;
but when a library is brought to such a degree of
perfection in any branch of science as this was in
Heraldry and History, both general and particular, I would have such a library preserved. 'Tis
said that he had some pique with the Heralds'
Office a little before his death, so cut them off
with a single book, otherwise he had left them the
whole of his library. And there not being much
money to spare amongst them, they do not appear
to possess themselves of any considerable share in
it. The Earl of Oxford, it is thought, will have
some sweep at it; but much of it is very likely to

---

[1] "A Catalogue of the valuable library collected by
that truly laborious Antiquary, Peter Le Neve, Esq. Norroy King of Arms (lately deceased), containing most of
the books relating to the History and Antiquities of
Great Britain and Ireland, and many other nations: with
more than a thousand Manuscripts of Abstracts of Records, &c., Heraldry, and other sciences, several of which
are very antient, and written on vellum: also, a great
number of Pedigrees of Noble Families, &c., with many
other curiosities; which will be sold by auction the 22nd
Feb. 1730-1, at the Bedford Coffee-house, in the Great
Piazza, Covent Garden, by John Wilcox, Bookseller in
Little Britain." This remarkable collection consisted of
nearly 1300 lots. It was followed by another sale on
March 19, 1730-1, of "Some Curiosities and Manuscripts
omitted in the previous Catalogue."

be divided among those who collect such rarities more through curiosity than use, and have neither purse nor abilities to make anything compleat with or from them. The Catalogue of the Heralds' Library is in print, containing 124 pages in 8vo.; and there is a Catalogue of all the books relating to Heraldry, set forth by Mr. Gore at Oxford, in quarto, 168-; it has, I think, had another impression.[2]

In the Prerogative Office there is a large collection of books all wrote on vellum, containing the wills and testaments of our forefathers, carefully preserved with calendars for the readier reference to their names.

The Bishops' Register Books are kept in each particular Register's Office.

The civilians of Doctors' Commons did about the year 1708 buy all the books of Common, Canon, and Civil Law in the great library of Dr. Oldys, then newly devised, which at his chambers filled three large rooms. They are ranged in a large room next the hall, and were then methodized by the learned Dr. Pinfold. I think they were above 1000 in number, besides some MSS.[3] They have made additional collections, and have a good catalogue of them.

The parochial churches have their registers of burials, christenings, and marriages. The halls of each company have also their registers of those they bind to trades or make free, and of their

---

[2] Thomas Gore's Catalogue of Writers upon Heraldry first appeared in 1668, and republished in 1674, 4to. with many additions by the author and his friends. It is a curious and useful book.

[3] Dr. William Oldys, the civilian, died at Kensington in 1708. "As a scholar," says Dr. Charles Coote, "he was respectable; as a civilian, he was learned; as a pleader, eloquent and judicious." The library of the College of Advocates, Doctors' Commons, was dispersed by Mr. Hodgson, on April 22, 1861, and seven following days.

masters, wardens, and their charters, granted by the several crowned heads, &c.

There are many records, books, and registers of the Hospital of the Charterhouse by what Mr. Hearne mentions in his account of that foundation.

CHRIST CHURCH, formerly the Grey Friars [Newgate Street], hath a neat library for the use of the masters and scholars, besides a collection of mathematical instruments, globes, ships, with all their rigging for the instruction of the lads designed for the sea[4]; and in their counting-house is the picture of Edward VI., their founder, said to be done by Hans Holbein[5]; and in the great hall a noble representation of King James II. sitting on his throne with most of the nobility, privy council, chancellor, governors, mayor and aldermen, and the boys and girls on their knees, all from the life by the famous Signior Verrio.[6]

---

[4] The Rev. Wm. Trollope, in his *History of Christ's Hospital*, 1834, p. 200., states that " in the mathematical school there is a library, considerably dilapidated indeed, but well worthy of preservation ; and devoutly is it to be hoped, that it may not, for want of due attention, meet with the same fate as the valuable astronomical apparatus, with which the observatory over the old school was furnished."

[5] At the upper extremity of the Court Room, under a canopy, with the arms of England over it, is the President's chair; behind which, in a panel, is a half-length portrait, by Holbein, of the Royal Founder. The painting is in good preservation ; and represents the young monarch in a standing position, with his left hand supported by the thumb fixed in his girdle, and the right holding a dagger with a blue tassel. He stands under a canopy of cloth of gold, fringed ; and is dressed in a crimson coat with half sleeves and basket-buttons, embroidered, and lined with ermine. By this portrait, Edward appears to have been of a fair and delicate complexion, with blue eyes, Grecian nose, full lips, and hair inclining to red. — *Trollope.*

[6] Verrio's picture on the north side of the Hall was

MERCHANT TAYLORS' SCHOOL and Mercers' Chapel School have their respective libraries similar to that of St. Paul's.

GRESHAM COLLEGE has a very good library, but depends on the Fellows of the Royal Society; those were mostly collected by that noble antiquary the Earl of Arundel. The MSS. he purchased in Germany, when he was ambassador to the Emperor's court, the journal of which was wrote by one Crowne of his lordship's retinue [7], though not so well performed as the nature of the subject deserved. These were the Remains of [Matthias Corvinus] King of Hungary, and afterwards fell into the hands of Bilibald Pirckeimer [8], where is to be seen his head graved by Albert Durer, one of the first examples among us of sticking or pasting of heads, arms, or ciphers into volumes. In this expedition he bought up all the rare books, statues, pictures, medals, and some entire libraries, with the remains of that at Heidelberg. A private MS. catalogue of these his German collections mentions also those presented him by the Duke of Saxony, particularly the drafts of his gold, silver, and copper medals performed by his own hands, in two volumes, with a very curious ancient MS., among others of Vitruvius. The earl's collections were given to that society by the Duke of Nor-

painted expressly for the Hospital, at the instigation of our amusing diarist, Mr. Samuel Pepys; but it was not without considerable trouble that the reluctant painter was induced to abide by his bargain.

[7] A True Relation of all the Remarkable Places and Passages observed in the Travels of the Lord Howard, Earl of Arundell and Surrey, in his Embassy to the Emperor Ferdinand II. By William Crowne. Lond. 1637. 4to. "A work full of imperfections and errors," says Oldys.

[8] Bilibald Pirckheimer, whose portrait was engraved by his friend Albert Durer in 1524, was a person of great authority in the city of Nuremberg. He published several works, and among others a humorous essay entitled

folk [9], and if a catalogue were taken according to
their merit, perhaps they could not be paralleled.
In the year 1687, Mr. Marmaduke Foster drew
up a catalogue, who was reputed to understand
printed books as well as most librarians in Europe;
but before it was printed it was thought fit to be
curtailed by some who knew nothing of the matter,
so that it is not Mr. Foster's catalogue. But he
was not so well skilled in ancient manuscripts, as
is evident by two Irish ones, which he saith were
the Picts' language. It deserves a representation
more accurate, the titles and descriptions of the
printed books being imperfect and unsatisfactory,
and the manuscripts intermixed and confused with
them [1]; nor in the large catalogue of MSS. printed
at Oxford [2] is justice done to those of this library.

Laus Podagræ — " The Praise of the Gout." He died in
1530, aged sixty.

[9] Evelyn, in his _Diary_, Aug. 29, 1678, says, " I was
called to London to wait upon the Duke of Norfolk, who
having at my sole request bestowed the Arundelian library on the Royal Society, sent to me to take charge of
the books. I procured for our Society, besides printed
books, near 100 MSS., some in Greek of great concern-
ment. The printed books being of the oldest impressions, are not the less valuable; I esteem them almost
equal to MSS. Amongst them are most of the Fathers,
printed at Basil, before the Jesuits abused them with
their expurgatory Indexes: there is a noble MS. of Vitruvius." In 1831, by mutual agreement, the Arundel
MSS. belonging to the Royal Society, with the exception
of the Oriental, were transferred to the British Museum.
The Oriental, about fifty in number, were not received
until the year 1835.

[1] Complete Catalogues of the Books, Manuscripts, and
Letters of the Royal Society were published in 1841.
They are sold to the Fellows and the public in two oc-
tavo volumes; one, containing the Scientific works, the
other, the Miscellaneous literature, MSS., and Letters.
A MS. Catalogue has also been made of the Maps, Charts,
Engravings, Drawings, &c., which exceed 5000 in num-
ber. (Weld's _Hist. of the Royal Society_, ii. 474.)

[2] Catalogi Librorum Manuscriptorum Angliæ et Hiberniæ, Oxon. 1697, fol. tom. ii. part. i. pp. 74-84.

In the College of Physicians in Warwick Lane is a fine collection, both in their own and other faculties. Mr. Selden bequeathed them his physical books, and the Marquis of Doncaster [Dorchester][3], one of their members, bestowed his whole collection upon them.

In WHITE CROSS STREET the library of Dr. Daniel Williams, left to the public, the Catalogue whereof makes a tolerable 8vo. volume.[4]

DUTCH CHURCH. In Austin Friars, in the remaining part of the conventual church used by the Dutch and Flemish to preach in, and allowed of in the reign of Edward VI. Over the door at the entrance is a library well furnished with books of divinity, and many original letters in MS. (never printed) of the first Reformers ; the printed books mostly Dutch. The Ten Commandments there are said to be written by the hand of Sir Peter Paul Rubens.[5]

---

[5] Henry Pierrepoint, Marquis of Dorchester, who was admitted a Fellow of the College of Physicians for his proficience in medicine and anatomy: ob. Dec. 8, 1680. Dr. Lort says he left his library to this college, containing a remarkably good collection of civil law books, the Catalogue of which has been published. Anthony Wood calls him "the pride and glory of the college." See Walpole's *Royal and Noble Authors*, by Park, iii. 229. Dr. Munk, in *The Roll of the Royal College of Physicians of London*, i. 262—274., has given an interesting notice of this distinguished nobleman. There is a Catalogue of this library, entitled " Bibliothecæ Collegii Regalis Medicorum Londinensis Catalogus." With an Appendix, 8vo. 1757.

[4] Catalogus Bibliothecæ Danielis Williams. 8vo. Lond. 1727. Editio secunda, 8vo. 1801. Appendix, 8vo. 1808, 1814; also in 2 vols. 8vo. 1841.

[5] On the west end over the skreen is a fair library, inscribed thus: ' Ecclesiæ Londino-Belgicæ Bibliotheca, extructa sumptibus Mariæ Dubois, 1659.' In this library are divers valuable MSS. and letters of Calvin, Peter Martyr, and others, foreign reformers. — Strype's *Stow*,

FRENCH CHURCHES.—In the French Church in Threadneedle Street [3], before the dreadful conflagration, was a library, and Minsheu mentions them to have subscribed for his *Dictionary*.[4] If this be true, then Mr. Ephraim Chambers is in the wrong when, in his *Cyclopædia*, he particularises Bp. Walton's *Polyglot Bible* to have been the first book that was published by subscription in England, an error he was led into by Anthony Wood.

The French congregation, that have a place of worship allowed them in part of the Hospital of the Savoy, have a library for the use of their ministry.

The Swedes have a church in Trinity Lane, and a collection there.

JEWS' SYNAGOGUE. — The Jews in their synagogue in Bevis Marks, near Duke's Place, have a collection relating to the ceremonial of their worship, the Talmud, and other Rabbinical learning. Their rolls, whereon the Pentateuch is written, are of fine calves' leather.[6] It is a fine building, though not comparable to that at Amsterdam.

---

b. ii. p. 116. Is Bagford quite correct in attributing the Decalogue in this church to Rubens? Wm. Sanderson, in his *Graphice*, p. 15., ed. 1658, informs us, that "King Charles's love to this art [painting] begat three knight-painters, Rubens, Vandyck, and Gerbier; the last had little of art or merit — a common pen-man, who pensil'd the Dialogue [Decalogue?] in the Dutch Church, London, his first rise of preferment." An interesting paper by the Rev. Thomas Hugo, on the early history of this house of the Augustine Friars, is printed in *The City Press* of Jan. 7, 1860.

[6] On what is now the site of the Hall of Commerce.

[7] "Mr. Ames has the paper or proposal Minsheu published with all the subscribers' names about the year 1629." (*Oldys.*) Minsheu appears to have printed the names of all the persons who took a copy of his *Dictionary*, and continually added to it, as purchasers came in.

[8] The great Synagogue, Duke's Place (now called St. James's Place), Aldgate, and the Spanish and Portuguese

FRIENDS' LIBRARY. — The Quakers have been
some years gathering a library, but where reposited
I hear not (but the Baptists have one at Barbi-
can.) One of their brethren named John Whiting, a man of good intelligence and assiduity, has
published a Catalogue of all the Friends' Books,
such as Naylor, written by that fraternity ; it
makes a moderate octavo, and was printed 1708.[9]
In my opinion 'tis more accurately and perfectly
drawn up than the Bodleian Library at Oxford is
by Dr. Hyde, for the Quaker does not confound
one man with another as the scholar does. Besides, the Quaker is so exact and satisfactory, that
he not only gives you the title ample enough, and
the size and the town where printed, but the
number of sheets or leaves every distinct Treatise contains, from the largest folio to the least
pamphlet ; and besides all that, what place every
author most considerable among them was of,
when and where he flourished, and died.
Francis Bugg, the notorious revolter from, and
scribbler against them, had the best collection of
their writings of any of the Brethren ; but I think
I have read in some of his rhapsodies that he
either gave or sold it to the library at Oxford.

Synagogue, between Nos. 10. and 11. Bevis Marks, have
in common a valuable library of Rabbinical and Jewish
literature, in a separate building close by. It ia in con-
templation to make this library a Beth Hammedrash, or
Hebrew College, with a view to the home education of
Jewish Rabbies for England, in preference to receiving
them from abroad. The library, which ia accessible to
stndents, haa a manuscript catalogue, and arrangements
for printing it are now in progress, but somewhat de-
layed.

[9] "A Catalogue of Friends' Books; written by many
of the People called Quakers, from the beginning or first
appearance of the said people. Collected for a General
Service, by J. W. [John Whiting.] London: Printed
and Sold by J. Sowle, in White Hart Court in Gracious
Street, 1708." 8vo. pp. 238.

DULWICH COLLEGE. — In Dulwich College,
erected by Alleyn the comedian, there is a library
to which Mr. Cartwright, a player[1], who was bred
a bookseller, and had a shop at the end of Turn-
stile Alley, gave a collection of plays[2], and also
many excellent pictures. There is to be seen a
View of London, taken by Norden in 1603, and
at the bottom of it a view of the Lord Mayor's
show.[3]

STATIONERS' COMPANY. — It were to be wished
the Stationers' Company would erect a library to
their Hall, it being commodiously enough situated
for resort from all parts ; and so many of them
having got estates by the learned, it would de-
monstrate some gratitude to the sciences, and

---

[1] William Cartwright, one of Killigrew's company at
the original establishment of Drury Lane. By his will,
dated 1686, he left his books, pictures, and furniture to
Dulwich College, where also his portrait still remains.

[2] " Here comes in the Queen's purchase of Plays; and
those by Mr. Weever, the dancing-master; Sir Charles
Cotterell, Mr. Coxeter, Lady Pomfret, and Lady Mary
Wortley Montagu." (Oldys.) It is clear from this note
that Oldys intended to enlarge this paper on the London
Libraries. See his Diary, antè p. 123.

[3] " Mr. Norden designed a View of London in eight
sheets, which was also engraved. At the bottom of this
was the representation of the cavalcade of the Lord
Mayor's show, all on horseback, the aldermen having
round caps on their heads. The View itself is singular,
and different from all that I have seen, and was taken by
Norden from the pitch of the hill towards Dulwich College going to Camberwell from London : in which college
on the stair-case I had a sight of it in company of Mr.
Christopher Brown. Mr. Secretary Pepys went afterwards to view it by my recommendation, and was very
desirous to have purchased it. But since it is decayed
and quite destroyed by means of the moistness of the
wall. This was made about the year 1604 or 1606 to the
best of my memory, and I have not met with any other
of the like kind." — Bagford's Letter to Hearne, Leland's
Collectanea, vol. i. p. lxxxii. See also " N. & Q.," 2nd S.
x. 372.

repay their expences sufficiently in honour and reputation. And this might easily be effected, if every one at first would give one book of a sort, and that of all pamphlets published weekly; six of a sort might be contributed here, to be sold or exchanged for bound or other books, reserving one of the pamphlets of a sort for the library. And here, that I am mentioning the most concise pamphlets or compositions, I must not pass by unobservant, Mr. Tomlinson's [Thomason's] most curious and costly collection of all the tracts or pamphlets that came out from 1640 to 1660. I think Bishop Kennett's *Historical Register* is an attempt of some abridgments in this nature, for he had a great collection, also a library of English Lives, Characters, &c.[4] But Tomlinson's [Thomason's] was so complete, and some of them so scarce, even within the time of that period, that King Charles I. (who encouraged his undertaking for the knowledge of posterity, which otherwise he had been soon weary of, through the great charge of collecting, danger of preserving, and difficulty of removing them from place to place out of the army's reach), wanting a certain small pamphlet, could get it nowhere. After strict inquiry, hearing where it was, he went to St. Paul's Churchyard and gave the bookseller ten pieces of gold only to read it (besides near 100 MSS. on the King's behalf, which nobody then dared print) in his own house.[5] This collection, containing near

---

[4] The valuable manuscript collections of the industrious Dr. White Kennett, Bishop of Peterborough in 107 volumes, chiefly relating to ecclesiastical history and biography, are in the Lansdowne collection in the British Museum.

[5] George Thomason, the loyal bookseller of the Rose and Crown, St. Paul's Churchyard, has been already noticed in "N. & Q." 1st Ser. vi. 175. 463. In the 2nd Ser. iv. 412., will be found some curious historical particulars of the remarkable preservation of this important

I

30,000 several pieces, is uniformly bound in
above 2000 volumes of all sizes, was so well digested, and every pamphlet referred to indivi-
dually, that the smallest tract of a single leaf might
be readily found therein, which was taken by Marmaduke Foster, the auctioneer, and is itself in
twelve volumes folio. For this collection the owner
is said to have refused four thousand pounds, yet
the present owner has not yet had, as I hear, above
three or two hundred pounds offered for them, and
that by the Duke of Chandos. After him, Miller [6]
was famous for his great store of pamphlets ; but
his Catalogue does not distinguish them more particularly than in bundles, so is useless to the
reader now they are disposed of. John Dunton [7]

- - - ———————————————

collection of pamphlets. It was commenced in the year
1641, and continued until 1662; arranged and bound in
chronological order in 2220 volumes, containing above
30,000 separate publications. Thomason died in 1666,
and in his Will at Doctors' Commons, these pamphlets
are particularly mentioned, and a special trust appointed,
Dr. Thomas Barlow, afterwards Bishop of Lincoln, being
one of the trustees. The 100 MSS., noticed by Oldys, are
bound up with the printed pamphlets in chronological
order. In 1647, Thomason published a Catalogue in 4to.
of his general stock, consisting of fifty-eight closely-
printed pages, entitled "Catalogus Librorum diversis
Italiæ locis Emptorum Anno Dom. 1647. A Georgio
Thomasono Bibliopola Londinensi apud quem in Cæmiterio D. Pauli ad insigne Rosæ coronatæ prostant venales.
Londini, Typis Iohannis Legatt, 1647." In the same year
a selection from this Catalogue was purchased by government; who ordained, that the sum of 500l. out of the
receipts at Goldsmiths' Hall should be paid to George
Thomason for a collection of books in the Eastern languages, lately brought out of Italy, that the same may
be bestowed upon the Public Library in Cambridge.
(*Journals of the House of Commons*, 24th Mar. 1647-8.)

[6] For John Dunton's characteristic notice of William
Miller, see Nichols's *Literary Anecdotes*, iii. 613., and
Timperley's *Dict. of Printing*, p. 739.

[7] Oldys probably alludes to John Dunton's *Athenianism, or New Projects*; being 600 distinct Treatises (in

also collected a great many pamphlets to repub-
lish the scarcest and most remarkable of them,
none of the meanest of his projects, had his judgment been answerable to his opportunities; but he
laid himself down no rule of confinement, so published two volumes of promiscuous and incoherent
things, and met with no encouragement to pro-
ceed any further.

Nor was the Collection of Historical and Political Pamphlets in my own little library perhaps
very contemptible, being above 5000.[8]

Mr. Roderick Mackenzie, who died a few years
since, had above 30,000 pamphlets.

HARLEIAN. — For libraries in more expressly
particular hands, the first and most universal in
England, must be reckoned the Harleian, or Earl
of Oxford's library, begun by his father and continued by himself. He has the rarest books of all
countries, languages, and sciences, and the greatest
number of any collector we ever had, in manu-

---

prose and verse). Lond. 1710, 8vo. In this first volume
you have (he says) twenty-four of those 600 projects
promised on the title. Nichols, iu his *Life of Dunton,*
p. xxv., gives a list of thirty-five projects which was to
form the second volume of the *Athenianism.*

[8] Bishop Kennett, in the Preface to his *Historical Register,* has wisely remarked, that " the bent and genius of
the age is best known in a free country by the pamphlets
and papers that come daily out, as the sense of parties,
and, sometimes, the voice of the nation." As supplying
materials of British history, Oldys duly estimated the
value of pamphlets to the historian and biographer, as is
obvious from his valuable " Dissertation upon Pamphlets,"
contained in J. Morgan's *Phœnix Britannicus,* 4to. 1732;
and his " Copious and Exact Catalogue of Pamphlets in
the Harleian Library," 4to., in which will be found many
curious particulars of literary and biographical history.
Of course Oldys's " Copious Catalogue " describes but a
very small portion of the Pamphlets formerly in this
noble library, which at one time it is estimated contained
350,000 distinct articles.

script as well as in print; thousands of fragments, some a thousand years old; vellum books, some written over; all things especially respecting English History, personal as well as local, particular as well as general. He has a great collection of Bibles, &c., in all versions, and editions of all the first printed books, classics, and others of our own country, ecclesiastical as well as civil, by Caxton, Wynkyn de Worde, Pynson, Berthelet, Rastall, Grafton, and the greatest number of pamphlets and prints of English heads of any other person. Abundance of ledgers, chartularies, old deeds, charters, patents, grants, covenants, pedigrees, inscriptions, &c., and original letters of eminent persons as many as would fill two hundred volumes; all the collections of his librarian Humphrey Wanley, of Stow, Sir Symonds D'Ewes, Prynne, Bishop Stillingfleet, John Bagford, Le Neve, and the flower of a hundred other libraries.[9]

Bishop Moore. — Dr. John Moore, the late Bishop of Ely, had also a prodigious collection of books, written as well as printed on vellum, some very ancient, others finely illuminated. He had a Capgrave's *Chronicle*, books of the first printing

---

[9] The first considerable purchase of books by Robert Harley, Earl of Oxford, was made in August, 1705, and which by means of agents abroad as well at home, at the time of his death, in 1724, was one of the most remarkable libraries in England. Edward, the second Earl, that noble patron of literature and learned men, continued to make additions with equal zeal and liberality. At his death on June 16, 1741, this noble collection included nearly 8,000 volumes of MSS.; about 50,000 volumes of printed books; 41,000 prints; and about 350,000 pamphlets. The printed books were purchased by Thomas Osborne for 13,000*l.* to be dispersed; but fortunately the collection of MSS., containing 7639 volumes, exclusive of 14,236 original rolls, charters, deeds, and other legal instruments, was purchased by government for the sum of 10,000*l.*

at Mentz, and other places abroad, as also at Oxford, St. Alban's, Westminster, &c. After his death his late majesty bought them for seven thousand pounds, and gave them to the University of Cambridge.[1]

EARL OF CLARENDON. — Henry Earl of Clarendon had a vast treasury of curiosities in this kind; he spent his whole time and substance too almost, I may say, upon inquiries and purchases of books and pamphlets, manuscripts, and medals; in the latter article whereof Mr. Evelyn was greatly beholden to his communications in the compiling his *Numismata* [Lond. fol. 1697.] Of some of his printed books, and such as were burnt at Cornbury, there are catalogues in print; but not of half the manuscripts he bought. For safety he reposited them in St. Martin's Library, then built by Archbishop Tenison, when Dr. Gibson, now Bishop of London, took a catalogue of them, which being styled *Tenisoniana* [2], a just offence was taken by the honourable owner, and as Dr. Rawlinson has observed, the MSS. were immediately removed.[3] This noble Earl bought all Sir James Ware's collection relating to Ireland, now in the possession

---

[1] Dr. John Moore, successively Bishop of Norwich and Ely, died 31st July, 1714. His curious and magnificent library, consisting of 30,755 volumes, was purchased in 1715 by George I. for 6,000 guineas, who presented it to the Public Library at Cambridge. It fills up the rooms on the north and west sides of the court over the philosophy and divinity schools, arranged in twenty-six classes. For memoranda of his printed books and MSS. see Addit. MSS. 5827. 6261. 6262., in the Brit. Museum. *Vide* Hartshorne's *Book Rarities in the University of Cambridge*, pp. 18-24.

[2] Dr. Gibson's Catalogue is entitled " Librorum Manuscriptorum in duabus insignibus Bibliothecis, altera Tenisoniana Londini, altera Dugdaliana Oxonii Catalogus. Oxon. 1692, 4to."

[3] *The English Topographer*, p. 115., 1720, 8vo.

I 3

of the Duke of Chandos.[4] He had abundance of
other manuscripts, ancient and modern, of which
I have seen many chests full, for he was an indefatigable collector, and held correspondence with
most of the learned and curious men of his time,
who were continually addressing him with some
historical or political observations and tracts or
others; but how scattered and consumed, most of
them I fear, it is a grief for me to think.[5] He
wrote many himself, and published some, but they
have not his name. He had great knowledge of
the history of the Peerage, Privileges, and Customs of Parliament, Prerogative, &c. Whilst
young, and with his father Sir Edward Hyde
abroad, he was much trained in reading, translating the epistolary intercourses of some of the most
eminent; (he) translated all Cardinal D'Ossat's
Letters into English[6], and I have seen the fair

[4] Sir James Ware's MS. collections relative to Ireland
were purchased of his heir by Henry, second Earl of
Clarendon, when lord-lieutenant in 1686, and after his
death by the Duke of Chandos. These underwent a
second dispersion by public auction, 1745-6. Dr. Milles,
Dean of Exeter, whose uncle had considerable property
in Ireland, purchased a large part, and deposited them in
the British Museum, Addit. MSS. 4755. to 4802. Of these
MSS. a Catalogue was printed at Dublin in 1648, and
again by Bernard, *Catalogi Librorum Manuscriptorum Angliæ et Hiberniæ*, tom. ii. part ii., p. 3., Oxon. 1697.

[5] See an interesting chapter on the fate of the Clarendon manuscripts in Lady Theresa Lewis's *Lives of the
Friends and Contemporaries of Lord Chancellor Clarendon*,
i. 65*-87.*

[6] Arnoldus D'Ossat, Cardinal Bishop of Rennes, and
afterwards of Bayeux. In the beginning of the reign of
Henry IV. he was sent to Rome to effect a reconciliation
between Clement VIII. and his royal master. He died
on March 13, 1604. His *Life*, by Madame Thiroux D'Ar-
conville, is in 2 vols. 8vo. Paris, 1771. Dr. Rawlinson
says, "The *Letters* of this great Cardinal contain all the
negociations relating to the affair of the absolution of
Henry IV.; and, according to the politicians, may be a
model to those who treat with the Court of Rome." The

copy of his own hand in a thick volume of above 1000 pages folio. His father then also engaged him to a translation of the Marquis de Rosny's negotiations in England, 1603, out of the *Memoirs* of the said Marquis, afterwards Duke of Sully, as the best rudiments of such knowledge as is necessary in the arts of government and negotiation. And indeed that account, though somewhat prolix, is the most copious, and gives the best light into the parties and factions, prospects and pursuits of the English Court, the best introduction to our history upon the succession of the Scottish line, of any that is to be found in all our own chronicles. At other times his father employed him as his amanuensis, and in transcribing his own correspondence, historical and political, particularly his *Essays and Discourses, Moral and Divine,* whereof during our domestic discords, he wrote many abroad, as he did afterwards also in his exile. The folio volume lately printed [7] contains not a quarter of the said Chancellor Clarendon's Remains, one of the most important of which, and that he principally designed for posthumous publication, was his own *Life*, fairly transcribed by his secretary Mr. Shaw, for the press, in near 200 pages folio ; but, through certain womanish fears of its throwing some odium on the memory of other persons, it has been denied the justice of clearing his own. From such laudable applications of the father, the son became such a lover of the like, that I have been assured by his own sister, the

best edition is that of 1708, *Lettres avec des Notes Historiques et Politiques de M. Amelot De la Houssaie,* Amst. 12mo. 5 vols.

[7] The Miscellaneous Works of the Right Hon. Edward, Earl of Clarendon ; being a Collection of several valuable Tracts written by that eminent Statesman, published from his Lordship's original MSS. fol. 1727, 1751. These tracts were obtained from the Chancellor's youngest daughter, Lady Frances Keightley.

Lady Francis Keightley, that he spent no less than an hundred thousand pounds upon the collections aforesaid.

THE EARL OF SUNDERLAND made an admirable collection of books in polite learning, particularly the rarest editions of the classicks, &c. The King of Denmark proffered his heirs thirty thousand pounds for it, and Queen Zara [8] would have inclined them to part with it; but for the honour of England it still retains those jewels [9], though it could not *that* jewel little regretted, which the French King gave twice that money for.[1] His Lordship bought the collection made by Mr. Adrian Beverland [2], which was very choice in its kind. This is undoubtedly the best way of gathering a library, especially if the collector was of our own profession, taste, &c. It saves a great deal of time, trouble, and money; for duplicates and subjects disregarded by one man will be as much another's choice; besides, this wholesale method often supplies the purchasers with many rarities he would otherwise never have known of, or might search to pick up singly in vain his whole life. This was the method taken by the Earl of Anglesey, who in the thirty years he disposed himself this way, bought

---

[8] Sarah, Duchess of Marlborough.

[9] Charles Spencer, third Earl of Sunderland (ob. April 19, 1722) was distinguished by his encouragement of learning and learned men. (*Spectator*, vol. vi. Dedication.) His library was removed to Blenheim in 1749, comprising upwards of 17,000 volumes, in various languages, arts, and sciences, all arranged in elegant cases, with gilt wire latticed doors.

[1] Probably an allusion to the Pitt diamond, purchased by the regent of France in 1717, as a jewel for the crown. Jeffreys says the price paid for it was 125,000l, other authors say 130,000l.

[2] Adrian Beverland, a classical scholar, memorable for his learning, the licentious character of his writings, and his contrition. He died about 1713.

several whole libraries, particularly that of Mr. Oldenburgh, Secretary of the Royal Society.[3] Hence his collection was so numerous; hence so universal, so extraordinary for its abundance, as well as scarcity thereof; hence such recourse, such acknowledgment thereunto by many persons of honour and learning, though possessed of very great libraries themselves, for the sight of many they could no where else see. But this, in October, 1686, was divided and dispersed again by an auction, as though it had never been, as appears by the Catalogue then printed in quarto, and published by Mr. Tho. Philipps, his Lordship's Gentleman.[4]

SIR HANS SLOANE has a very large Collection of Books in all faculties and languages, old printed books and manuscripts, whereof he has about 3000 volumes, and above 1200 of them in folio. Above all, his library is one of the most complete in Travels, Voyages, and Natural His-

---

[3] Henry Oldenburgh, a mathematician and natural philosopher, born in 1626, and died in 1678. *Vide* Wood's *Fasti*, (Bliss); Martin's *Biog. Philosophica*, p. 109; Worthington's *Diary*, i. 192; *Gent. Mag.* li. 629; Nichols's *Lit. Anec.* iv. 442; and "N. & Q." 2nd S. vi. 270.

[4] Arthur Annesley, first Earl of Anglesey of that family: ob. April 6, 1686. The Catalogue of his library is entitled "Bibliotheca Anglesiana, sive Catalogus variorum librorum in quâvis linguâ, et facultate insignium: quos cum ingenti sumptu et summâ diligentiâ sibi procuravit Honoratiss. Arthur Comes D'Anglesey, Privati olim Sigilli Custos, et Carolo Secundo à Secretioribus Conciliis. Quorum Auctio habebitur Londini, in Ædibus Nigri Cygni ex adverso Australis Porticus Ecclesiæ Cathed. Paulin in Cæmiterio D. Paul. 25 die Octob. 1686. Per Thomam Philippum, Generosum, olim Oeconomum prædicto Comiti. 4to. 1686." This sale is memorable for the discovery of the Earl's note on the fly-leaf of a copy of Εἰκων Βασιλικη, attributing this work to Bishop Gauden, which occasioned a keen controversy.

tory in Europe. A large museum of natural and
artificial rarities, as shells, jewels, fossils, plants,
animals, medals, antique and modern, Roman and
Greek antiquities, ores of all sorts, a vast quantity
of which had been collected by that great virtuoso
Mr. William Charleton [5], consisting together of
the greatest variety in England. He has great
books of plants, all exotic and native; an extraordinary collection of voyages, travels, and discoveries in most European languages; many
manuscripts never printed, in Latin, Italian,
Spanish, French, German, Dutch, Flemish, and
English.[6]

Dr. Mead has also a renowned library, some
of which he picked up at Rome many years ago,
and industriously made improvements ever since.[7]

The Earl of Carbury has a noble collection;
amongst them many relating to mystical divinity.

The Earl of Kent has spared for no cost to
collect a library of English history, journals of
parliament, visitations, pedigrees, &c.

---

[5] Evelyn, in his *Diary*, Dec. 16, 1687, says, " I carried the Countess of Sunderland to see the rarities of
one Mr. Charlton [Courten is the family name] in the
Middle Temple, who showed us such a collection as I
had never seen in all my travels. It consisted of miniatures, drawings, shells, insects, medals, animals, minerals,
precious stones, &c. This gentleman's Collection is estimated at 8,000*l*." See also for Evelyn's second visit,
Mar. 11, 1690.

[6] Sir Hans Sloane died on the 11th Jan. 1753. His
collections, now in the British Museum, were purchased
by parliament for 20,000*l*. His MSS. consist of 4100
volumes, of which a Catalogue was compiled by Samuel
Ayscough, 2 vols. 4to. 1782.

[7] Richard Mead, M.D. died on Feb. 16, 1754. The
sale of his library in Nov. and Dec. 1754, lasted for fifty-
seven days, and realised 5518*l*. 10*s*. 11*d*.: his pictures,
coins, and other antiquities, 10,550*l*. 18*s*.

The EARL OF PEMBROKE [8] is stored with antiquities relating to medals, lives, also with seals,
figures, busts and sculptures in marble and in
precious stones.

The LORD SOMERS's collection consisted in the
laws of this and other nations in various languages,
and of our own English historians, both printed
and in manuscript. I think they are now in the
custody of Sir Joseph Jekyl, Master of the Rolls,
who being now dead, they are to be sold by auction.[9]

The LORD HALIFAX[1] made an excellent collection ; they were well chosen and well digested.

The DUKE OF KINGSTON has also a very numerous and valuable library, whereof he has printed
a Catalogue.[2] The Lord Hay[3] has also made
many curious collections for several years past.

---

[8] Henry Herbert, ninth Earl. *Vide* Nichols's *Literary
Anecdotes. passim.*
[9] John Lord Somers died on the 26th of April, 1716.
Addison dedicated to him the first volume of the *Spectator.* The collection called the *Somers Tracts*, first
printed in 1748, in sixteen volumes, 4to., and again in
1809—15, in thirteen volumes, 4to., edited by Sir Walter
Scott, consists of scarce pamphlets selected principally
from the library of Lord Somers. A valuable collection
of original letters and other papers left by his lordship
was consumed in a fire which happened in the Chambers of the Hon. Charles Yorke in Lincoln's Inn Square,
on the 29th Jan. 1752.
[1] Charles Montagu, created Earl of Halifax, and
Viscount Sunbury, co. Middlesex, 14th Oct. 1714: ob.
1715.
[2] Evelyn Pierrepoint, the first Duke: ob. 1726. The
Catalogue of his library made seventy-seven sheets of
folio, of which only twenty copies were printed. It is
adorned with head and tail pieces of the Duke's house,
library, gardens, &c.
[5] George Henry Hay, of Pedwardine, afterwards the
7th Earl of Kinnoul in Scotland: ob. 1758.

His Lordship has also large and well chosen collections in Civil Law and Mathematics. The Lord
Colerain and Bishop Kennett had a library of
lives.

RICHARD SMYTH.—For persons of inferior rank,
we never had one more successful in his time for
picking up whatsoever was valuable and scarce,
and in such variety or abundance, than Mr. Henry
[Richard] Smyth, Secondary of the Poultry Comp-
ter. There was no day passed over his head in
which he visited not Moorfields, Little Britain, or
Paul's Churchyard; and for many years together
suffered nothing to escape him that was rare and
remarkable. He had laid in a good stock of acquaintance with all our writers and eminent men;
knew their characters and their compositions, and,
therefore, how much from time to time he wanted
to make any argument, controversy, &c., complete. He had pamphlets as valuable as manuscripts; was an author, as well as a buyer of
books : but they fell to the auctioneer, Richard
Chiswell, at last, in May, 1682 ; and were sold at
the Swan in Bartholomew Close. So no footstep
of this extraordinary library remains, which makes
perhaps the richest Catalogue of any private library we have to show in print, making above
400 pages in a very broad-leaved and close
printed quarto.[4]

MR. SECRETARY PEPYS was a great virtuoso in
collections of this nature ; they consisted much in
English History, both by land and sea, much relating to the Admiralty and maritime affairs. He

---

[4] Richard Smyth's interesting *Obituary* has been edited
by Sir Henry Ellis for the Camden Society. For notices
of this collector, consult "N. & Q." 1st S. ii. 389. ; 2nd S.
iii. 112. ; and viii. 87. The Sale Catalogue of Smyth's
library, with manuscript prices, is now in the British
Museum.

collected very much from the Records in the
Tower ; had many tine models and new inven-
tions of ships and historical paintings of them —·
as the drawing of Henry VIII.'s navy ; had many
books of mathematics and other sciences : many
costly curiosities relating to the City of London—
as views, maps, palaces, churches, coronations,
funerals, mayoralties, habits, heads of all our
famous men, drawn as well as printed ; the most
complete of anything in its kind. He had also
the copies and writing books of many dexterous
calligraphers ; the best collection in Europe, except perhaps Mr. Robert More's, who succeeded
to Col. John Ayres, his collection as well as his
business in Paul's School for some years. A man
whose free and generous spirit appeared in his
pen, and his ingenious fancy at his finger's end.
Mr. Pepys collected also many graved devices,
title-pages, and frontispieces of foreign as well as
domestic gravers, much augmented by his nephew
and Mr. Jackson. With many other curious collections, disposed very⁶methodically for the easy
finding any author on any subject, and the least
piece as soon as the largest.⁵ No catalogue is

---

⁵ The Pepysian library at Magdalene College is admirably described by the Rev. C. H. Hartshorne in *The
Book Rarities in the University of Cambridge*, pp. 219—
269. Consult also Nichols's *Literary Anecdotes*, iv. 550.,
and *The Diary and Correspondence of Samuel Pepys*,
Index. When may we expect a good biographical account of this remarkable man? Owing to the increasing
weakness of his eyes, Pepys concluded his *Diary* with
these memorable words : "And so I betake myself to that
course, which is almost as much as to see myself go into
my grave: for which, and all the discomforts that will
accompany my being blind, the good God prepare me!"
This was written on the 31st of May, 1669, but his death
did not take place until the 26th of May, 1703; so that
for a period of thirty-four years, comparatively little is
known of his personal history and connexion with the
republic of letters. We believe that the Life of Samuel

perhaps now perfect except the Lord Maitland's,
digested by his own direction; containing the
author's name, place where printed, printer's
name, date, and subject-matter contained in the
book, which must be of great use to the possessors.[6] Catalogues of this nature would give us
very great intelligence in a little time.

The various tastes and pursuits of curious men
in their collections of this kind, would be divert-
ing to a satirical genius, when we know that the
famous Dryden, and also Mr. Congreve after him,
had collected some volumes of old ballads and
penny story books. Mr. Hearne had the like.[7]
There's an author alive, I may venture to name
him, 'tis Mr. Robert Samber, who would needs
turn virtuoso too, and have his collection ; which
was, of all the printed tobacco papers he could
anywhere light of.[8] The conjunction made them
more observable :

"Et quæ non prosnnt singula, multa juvant."

Pepys has more than once been the topic of conversation
in the literary gatherings in Albemarle Street.

[6] Richard Maitland, fourth Earl of Lauderdale, whose
translation of Virgil, while it remained in manuscript,
was read and praised by Dryden. His Catalogue is entitled "Catalogus Librorum instructissimæ Bibliothecæ
Nobilis cujusdam Scoto-Britanni in quâvis linguâ et
facultate insignium: quibus adjicitur figurarum manu-
delineatarum, necnon tabularum ære incisarum per ce-
loberrimos Artis Chalcographicæ Magistros, Collectio
refertissima. Quorum Auctio habenda est Londini, ad
insigne Ursi in vico (vulgò dicto) Ave Mary-lane, propè
Ludgate-street, octavo die Aprilis, 1689, per Benj. Wal-
ford, Bibliop. Lond." It makes 150 closely-printed
pages in 4to.

[7] In addition to Pepys's five folio volumes of curious
Old Ballads, and the two large folio volumes of prints
and drawings to illustrate the history of London, he made
a collection in four duodecimo volumes (mostly in black-
letter) of Penny Merriments, Penny Witticisms, Penny
Compliments, and Penny Godlinesses, each volume containing about a thousand or fifteen hundred pages.

[8] See ' N. & Q." 2nd S. xi. 502.

But that which is often begun in whim and hu-
mour, custom will by degrees turn to serious application and solicitude, and so it has proved here.
But enough of this.

MR. WILD, who formerly lived in Bloomsbury,
had a good collection in husbandry and architec-
ture: so had MR. EVELYN. A certain Templar
one of astrology, witchcraft, and magic.

MR. THOMAS BRITTON, the small-coal man in
St. John's, Clerkenwell, had an excellent collection of chemical books, as appears by the printed
Catalogue, when they were sold by auction. He
had also a great parcel of music books, many of
them pricked with his own hand.[9]

---

[9] At the death of Britton, his valuable collection of
music sold for nearly 100*l.* In a mezzotinto print taken
by Woolaston, Britton is represented tuning a harpsichord,
a violin hanging on the side of the room, and shelves of
books before him. To this print are the following lines
by Prior: —

"Tho' doom'd to Small Coal, yet to arts ally'd,
    Rich without wealth, and famous without pride;
Music's best patron, judge of books and men,
    Belov'd and honour'd by Apollo's train;
In Greece or Rome, sure never did appear,
    So bright a genius in so dark a sphere;
More of the man had artfully been sav'd,
    Had KNELLER painted, and had VERTUE grav'd."

Bagford and Britton used frequently to indulge in a
literary chit-chat on old books and old manuscripts, and
both agreed to retrieve what fragments of antiquity they
possibly could. We have before us the Sale Catalogue of
the Small Coal-Man's library, and a curious one it is,
containing just such an inventory of literary relics as
would have mightily pleased old Anthony Wood, Tom
Hearne, and Browne Willis. It consists of forty closely-
printed pages in quarto, and entitled "The Library of
Mr. Thomas Britton, Small-Coal Man: being a curious
Collection of Books in Divinity, History, Physick, and
Chimistry, in all volumes; also, an extraordinary Collection of Manuscripts in Latin and English, will be

Dr. Beaumont collected all about mystical divinity and spirits. Mr. C. T. P., &c., &c., collections of feigned miracles, visions, prophecies, revelations, possessions, and pious impostures of all kinds. Captain Aston, of voyages and travels in most of the European languages, as well as some on other subjects. Sir Andrew Fountain, antiquities, prints, and medals. Mr. Serjeant Surgeon Bernard, the fairest and best editions of the classics in all volumes; and Mr. Dobbins, a good collection of surgery. Mr. Huckle, on Tower Hill, of modern authors in all languages; had great knowledge, and made a good choice of copper prints. Mr. Graham, Mr. Child, Mr. Chicheley, Mr. Walter Clavell of the Temple, have been noted for their collections both in print and MS. This last bought Giordano's book[10], and gave it one of the Universities to be answered.

Mr. Bridges's choice and valuable library was lately disposed of in Lincoln's Inn, the Catalogue whereof makes a handsome bound octavo volume. He had a collection of Wenceslaus Hollar's etchings in four volumes, and they containing not all his performances, which sold there for above 100l.[1]

---

sold by Auction at Tom's Coffee-house, adjoyning to Ludgate, on Thursday the 1st of November [1715], by John Bullord."

[10] Giordano Bruno's *Spaccio de la Bestia Trionfante,* Paris, 1584, noticed in *The Spectator,* No. 389. Vide Nichols's *Literary Anecdotes,* ii. 593.; iv. 105.

[1] Bridges's Catalogue is entitled "Bibliothecæ Bridgesianæ Catalogus: or, A Catalogue of the entire Library of John Bridges, late of Lincoln's Inn, Esq., consisting of above 4000 Books and Manuscripts in all languages and faculties, particularly in Classics and History, and especially the History and Antiquities of Great Britain and Ireland, which will begin to be sold by Auction on Monday, 7th Feb. 1725-6, at his Chambers in Lincoln's Inn, No. 6." 8vo. pp. 199. It realised 4160l. 12s. Hearne in his *Diary,* under Feb. 15, 1725-6, says "My late friend

The late Mr. Thomas Rawlinson has been the greatest collector of books in our time who has made his collections public ; for before his death, as well as since, they have been sold by auction. I think there have been seventeen or eighteen large catalogues sold off from the 4th of Dec. 1721, when his first auction began at Paul's Coffee House, to the 4th of March, 1733, when the last auction of his books including his MSS. began at the same place, and the books are not all gone out of London House yet; but he out of one volume made many, and all the tracts or pamphlets that came to his hands in volumes and bound together, he separated to sell them singly, so that what some curious men had been pairing and sorting half their lives to have a topic or argument complete, he by this means confused and dispersed again. He's called Tom Folio in the *Tatlers.* If his purse had been much wider he had a passion be-yond it, and would have been driven to part with what he was so fond of, such a pitch of curiosity or dotage he was arrived at upon a different edition, a fairer copy, a larger paper, than twenty of the same sort he might be already possessed of. In short, his covetousness after those books he had not increased with the multiplication of those he had ; and as he lived so he died, in his bundles, piles, and bulwarks of paper, in dust and cobwebs, at London House in Aldersgate Street.[2]

John Bridges, Esq.'s books being now selling by auction in London (they began to be sold on Monday the 7th inst.), 1 hear they go very high, being fair books, in good condition, and most of them finely bound. This afternoon 1 was told of a gentleman of All Souls' College, (I suppose Dr. Clarke,) that gave a commission of 8s. for an Homer in 2 vols., a small 8vo. if not 12mo. But it went for six guineas. People are in love with good bind-ing more than good reading."

[2] Thomas Rawlinson at first lived in Gray's Inn, where he had four chambers so completely filled with books, that his bed was removed into the passage. He afterwards

Several more might be named who have been
famous for their libraries, as Thomas Sclater Bacon, Esq., whose collection amounted in the catalogue to 12,000, besides his vast quantities of
prints, pamphlets, &c., begun to be sold by Cock
the auctioneer, under the Piazza in Covent Garden, 14 March, 1736-7.[3] Mr. West of Lincoln's
Inn, Sir Thos. Sebright, Mr. Calamy, Mr. Rawlinson, the apothecary, whose library sold to a
bookseller for above 1000*l.*; Mr. Jones's mathematical library, Mr. Constable of Yorkshire, Mr.
Granger, Mr. Topham, famous for his Greek collections, prints, and drawings ; Dr. Goodman, Dr.
Gray, Dr. Tyson, and Dr. Woodward. Mr. Good-
win of Pinder had a valuable library, and Dr.
Salmon the largest collection of English folios in
any private hands, being near 2000 in number,

---

resided at London House in Aldersgate Street, where he
died on August 6, 1725, aged 44. At that time his library contained the largest collection of books which had
ever been offered to the public. The Catalogue of his
printed books consists of nine parts; and the sale of his
manuscripts alone lasted for sixteen days. This biblio-
polist was certainly a remarkable man, in spite of Addison's satirical notice of him in No. 158. of *The Tatler.*
Tom Hearne thought very highly of him. " Some gave
out, (he says) and published it too in printed papers, that
Mr. Rawlinson understood the editions and title-pages of
books only, without any other skill in them, and there-
upon they styled him TOM FOLIO. But these were only
buffoons, and persons of very shallow learning. 'Tis certain that Mr. Rawlinson understood the editions and
titles of books better than any man I ever knew (for he
had a very great memory); but then besides this, he was
a great reader, and had read abundance of the best writers, ancient and modern, throughout, and was entirely
master of the learning contained in them. He had digested the classicks so well as to be able readily and upon
all occasions (what I have very often admired) to make
use of passages from them very pertinently, what I never
knew in so great perfection in any other person whatsoever." —*Diary*, Sept. 4, 1725.
    [3] See *antè*, pp. 18, 19.

with quartos and octavos proportionable. Mr. Anthony Collins had the largest collection of controversial pamphlets, which are specified in two thick
octavo catalogues.

Now that I have mentioned the largest, let's not
forget the least compositors.

Old JOHN MURRAY of Sacomb has made scarce
publications of English authors his inquiry all his
life: he has been a collector above forty years at
all sales, auctions, shops, and stalls, partly for his
own curiosity, and partly to oblige such authors
and gentry as have commissioned him. His account of any old English book as to the complete-
ness, scarcity, value, and general character of it,
has always been regarded by Mr. Anstis, Hearne,
Le Neve, and many other knowing antiquaries,
who were better judges of the subject matter of
these books than himself.[4]

---

[4] Hearne has the following notices of this literary antiquary in his *Diary* : — " Aug. 23, 1726. Mr. Murray
told me formerly that he began to collect books at eleven,
now he says at thirteen, years of age. I thought Mr.
Murray had kept all his curiosities together, ever since
he began collecting, excepting duplicates; but he tells
me now, that besides duplicates, he hath parted, upon occasion, with a vast number of things, and I find he lets
any one that wants have what books he hath, and 'tis
this way that he gets his support.

" Feb. 25, 1734-5. Mr. West, in his letter of the 17th
inst. from the Inner Temple, tells me he had a little before been fetch'd to Sacombe in Hertfordshire, by a mes-
senger, to our honest friend John Murray. He is in a
very declining way, occasioned by a slow fever, acquired
by overheating his blood in his last walk from London
thither, which is looked upon as twenty miles.

" Ap. 1, 1735. Mr. John Murray, who was very dan-
gerously ill lately at Sacombe in Hertfordshire, is since
gone to London (as Mr. West in his letter of March 17,
1734-5,) much recovered, so that 'twas hoped he got
strength daily."

John Murray was born on January 24, 1670, and died
Sept. 13, 1748. Dr. Rawlinson possessed a painting of

We have several parsons, I see too, who begun
to turn the penny this way, and what with chop-
ping and changing, and selling and buying, appear to be great customers and friends to the
muses.

The booksellers abroad may be more learned,
and make better judgment of their books, than
ours, but I believe few are better stored. I have
known several of them mark at auctions in their
catalogues the prices that books go off at, and so
settle a value on their own to persons conform-
ably, which is a most erroneous valuation, to make
a general rule of a particular inclination or necessity. I have given myself twenty shillings for a
thing that is worth to no other man, I believe, a
tenth part of that money, nor to me after I had
some little circumstance out of it. The atheisti-
cal book of Giordano Bruno sold at Paul's Coffee
House for 30l. in 1709; it has scarcely sold for so
many pence since.[5] And a complete Holinshead
rose there some years after to 80l.; it has never
sold again for so many shillings. The value of it
was thought to lie in its being complete; but now
the castrated sheets are reprinted you may have
many of the books complete, yet they will bear
no extravagant valuation: therefore the value
arose neither from a desire of knowledge which the

---

him, which was engraved by Vertue. He is leaning on
three books, inscribed " T. Hearne, V. III. Sessions
Papers, and Tryals of Witches," and holding a fourth
under his coat. Underneath are the following lines,
signed G. N.: —

" Oh ! Maister John Murray of Sacomb,
 The works of Old Time to collect was his pride,
  Till Oblivion dreaded his care :
 Regardless of friends intestate he died,
 So the rooks and the crows were his heirs."

[5] Probably his *Spaccio de la Bestia Trionfante*, Paris,
1584. *Vide* Nichols's *Liter. Anecdotes*, ii. 593.; iv. 105.,
and *ante*, p. 100.

scarce part would communicate, neither from its intrinsic remarkableness or instruction, nor even from any use to be made of it, but merely from the empty property of singularity, and being, as the contending purchasers erroneously thought, no where to be found. If there were no foolish bidders, there would be no extortionate sellers of books; but Tom Guy had seen enough into the course of business to justify the propriety of founding an hospital for incurables, though he might not have so grateful a meaning therein towards some of the authors and purchasers who helped to make him so rich, because he might be apprehensive that their condition at worst might be happier than his, inasmuch as it is more miserable to starve in the midst of riches than in the privation of them.[6]

But if we consider the stores of our booksellers (it having been frequent with some of them to make sales of 5000 books at a time, for others to have gotten clear 300*l*. or 400*l*. by a sale and one showed me of many, lately in Gray's Inn Hall, which he had the liberty of sorting them in, as he did assure me, were about 40,000 in number), we shall find occasion to believe we exceed many foreign

---

[6] Thomas Guy was the son of a lighterman at Horsleydown, where he was born in 1644. He was apprenticed on Sept. 2, 1660, to John Clarke, bookseller, in the porch of Mercers' Hall, Cheapside. In this house, rebuilt after the Great Fire, he commenced business for himself; but subsequently removed to a shop in the angle formed by Cornhill and Lombard Street, since known as " The Lucky Corner." Mr. Guy represented the borough of Tamworth in parliament from 1695 to 1707, his mother's native place. He is said to have made his fortune ostensibly by the sale of Bibles; but more, it is thought, by purchasing seamen's tickets, and by the sale and transfer of stock in the memorable South Sea year of 1720. The building and furnishing of his Hospital amounted to 18,792*l*. 16*s*.; and the endowment to 219,499*l*. He died on the 27th Dec. 1724, in the 80th year of his age.

traders in this commodity. For, except a few of
our most noted Latin authors, we send but few
abroad, and English books are as little read there
as Dutch are here. But, on the other hand, we
have great importations every year from abroad,
especially France and Holland, of books in all
faculties, and in all languages, by Vaillant, Van-
denboeck, Prevost, and Denoyere. I believe
James Woodman and his partner imported a thousand pounds' worth every year. He also got over
all the foreign books that anyways treated of our
country or its natives, stained with prejudice indeed many of them, no disturbance perhaps to
him, because written by opposites in religion,
nevertheless acceptable and useful to us, as he
found by the advantage be made of them.

For these and other reasons, flowing from the
liberty of the press, it may be that such a man as
Christopher Bateman may have had more books
gone through his hands than any bookseller in
Paris, he having bought and sold so many libraries
for nearly fifty years together. His office or shop
hath been the magazine from whence many of the
gentlemen before mentioned have constantly supplied themselves. No wonder our nation abounds
so in books, and we meet with such numerous
libraries wherever we turn, since we have some
to increase, and so few outlets of them. The
library of Vossius did indeed escape through some
sinister management as it is thought. A few upon
Trade, Travels, and Navigation have gone to the
Plantations; and a few are sometimes sold by
ignorant women to grocers, chandlers, and trunk-
makers, but few are so ignorant as not to know
if the books they cannot read or want money for
are perfect, that the booksellers will give more
money for them. The best defence I know of for
to keep the ignorant from laying violent hands on
the works of the learned and preserve the inside
of a book is to deck the outside finely. And

though a wise man is not captivated with externals, yet he knows that finery will breed esteem
and veneration in fools. See what the learned
Gassendus says of Peiresc in his life. On this
topic of bookbinding a greater deference should
be paid to good manuscripts, which on the cont ·ary I seldom meet with well bound. Whether
oe authors, intending a second and fairer copy,
hink anything good enough to contain the first,
or whether they modestly decline to show any ostentatious regard to their own compositions I know
not ; but so it is, that they commonly make such
a contemptible figure to the eye, both with outside
and within, that I am persuaded the foul and
slovenly writing, and the greasy parchment or
paltry paper covering of them, has promoted the
disregard and destruction of some of the finest
performances of our forefathers.

As for the auctioneers, I know not the name of
the first amongst us, not having seen the catalogue of Dr. Seaman's books, which were the first
that were published by auction [7], however An-

---

[7] Dr. Seaman's Catalogue is entitled "Catalogus Variorum et Insignium Librorum instructissimæ Bibliothecæ
Clarissimi Doctissimique Viri Lazari Seaman, S. T. D.
Quorum Auctio habebitur Londini in ædibus Defuncti in
Area et Viculo Warwicensi, Octobris ultimo. Cura Gulielmi Cooper, Bibliopolæ, 1676. 4to. pp. 137." Dr. Seaman's residence was in Warwick Court, in Warwick Lane.
In the Preface to the Reader, the auctioneer states, "It
hath not been usual here in England to make Sale of Books
by way of Auction, or who will give most for them; but
it having been practised in other countries to the advantage both of buyers and sellers, it was therefore conceived
(for the encouragement of learning) to publish the sale of
these books this manner of way; and it is hoped that this
will not be unacceptable to scholars; and therefore we
thought it convenient to give an Advertisement concerning the manner of proceeding therein."
Hearne thus notices this sale: "Feb. 13, 1722-3. The
first catalogue of books sold by auction was the library
of Dr. Seaman; the second was that of the Rev. Mr.

thony Wood mistook Mr. Smith's to be so.   Those
that have been most conspicuous were Dunmore,
Ned Millington, of whom there is a poem in Tom
Brown's posthumous Works[9], Marmaduke Foster,
Cooper, Bullard, &c., who have had vast quanti-
ties pass through their hands, as Smith's, Lord An-

Thomas Kidner, A.M., Rector of Hitchin in Hartford-
shire, beginning Feb. 6, 1676-7." On the progress of selling books by catalogues, see an article by Mr. Gough in
Nichols's *Literary Anecdotes*, iii. 608. ; and Dibdin's *Bibliomania*, 402. 408. 418., &c.   In the British Museum is a
quarto volume containing the first eleven Catalogues of
Books sold by auction with the prices in manuscript,
namely, those of 1. Seaman, 31 Oct. 1676.   2. Kidner,
Feb. 1676-7.   3. Greenhill, Feb. 1677-8.   4. Manton,
March, 1678.   5. Worsley, May, 1678.   6. Godolphin and
Phillips, Nov. 1678.   7. Voetius, Nov. 1678.   8. Sanger
and Brook, Lord Warwick, Dec. 1678.   9. Apud Theatrum Sheldonianum, Feb. 1678-9.   10. Watkins and
Sherley, June, 1679.   11. Bishe, Nov. [1679?]   To this
volume Mr. Heber has added the following MS. note : "This
volume, which formerly belonged to Narcissus Luttrell,
and since to Mr. Gough, is remarkable for containing the
eleven first Catalogues of Books ever sold by auction in
England.   What renders it still more curious, is that the
prices of nearly all the articles are added in MS.   When
it came into my possession it had suffered so much from
damp, and the leaves were so tender and rotten, that
every time the volume was opened, it was liable to injury.
This has been remedied by giving the whole a strong
coat of size.   At Willett's sale, Booth the bookseller of
Duke Street, Portland Place, bought a volume of old Catalogues for 2*l.* 3*s.* (see Merly Catalogue, n. 531.), and
charged the same in his own shop Catalogue for 1815
21*l.* (lot 6823).   It contained merely the eight which
stand first in the present collection, of which Greenhill's
and Godolphin's were not priced at all ; and Voet's and
Sanger's only partially.   However, it enabled me to fill
up a few omissions in the prices of my copy of Sanger's.
N.B. The prices of Willett's and the present copy did not
always tally exactly."   At the sale of Heber's Library this
volume sold for 3*l.*

[9] See the *Works* of Mr. Thomas Brown, ed. 1744, vol.
iv. p. 320., for " An Elegy on the Death of Mr. Edward

glesey's [9], Dr. Jacomb's, Earl of Ailsbury's, Lord Maitland's, and those vast stocks of Scots and Davis's of Oxford, with many others that has much improved the curious, and let them into a knowledge and value of what before lay dusty and disposed in studios, warehouses, and lumber-rooms.

But the better to know what we may inquire after and what is to be had, we should consult the catalogues of what have been amassed and is dispersed, or what still continues entire and unseparated. France, Spain, Italy, &c., spare no cost and pains to illustrate, and set forth their collections; and if we were not wanting of encouragement here, we have as able hands, as noble collections, and as great a variety as any part of Europe. But what numbers of useful and valuable books are imprisoned and concealed from the world by the jealous or covetous temper of some possessors! How much is Science impeded and prejudiced, mankind kept in the dark, and our country dishonoured, so contrary to the spirit of communication which men as men and sociable creatures, much more those of knowledge, ought to be endowed with, by not exhibiting catalogues of their libraries to the world, or permitting the ingenious to have recourse to them.

Millington, the famous Auctioneer." To the Elegy is subjoined the following Epitaph : —

" Underneath this marble stone
Lives the famous Millington :
A man who through the world did steer,
I' th' station of an auctioneer ;
A man with wond'rous sense and wisdom blest,
Whose qualities are not to be exprest."

[9] See *antè*, p. 93.

L

INDEX.

THE END.

LONDON
PRINTED BY SPOTTISWOODE AND CO.
NEW-STREET SQUARE

www.ingramcontent.com/pod-product-compliance
Lightning Source LLC
Chambersburg PA
CBHW020232030726
47497CB00009B/3061